R0110788965

01/2019

SET MI   D1338360

SALVATORE STRIANO was born in 1972 in Naples. During a stint in prison he discovered a love of reading and theatre. Striano is now a successful actor and has had a number of roles in cinema and television, including *Gomorra* and *Cesare deve morire*, based on Shakespeare's *Julius Caesar.*

BRIGID MAHER was born in Lucca and spent part of her childhood there. She has translated several Italian novels and is currently Senior Lecturer in Italian Studies at La Trobe University in Melbourne.

SET ME FREE

THE STORY OF HOW
SHAKESPEARE SAVED A LIFE

SALVATORE STRIANO

TRANSLATED FROM THE ITALIAN
BY BRIGID MAHER

TEXT PUBLISHING MELBOURNE AUSTRALIA

textpublishing.com.au

The Text Publishing Company
Swann House
22 William Street
Melbourne Victoria 3000
Australia

First published in Italian as *La Tempesta di Sasà* in 2016 by Chiarelettere
First published in English by The Text Publishing Company in 2017

Book design by Jessica Horrocks
Cover based on the original Giacomo Callo / Marina Pezzotta / Chiarelettere design
Cover illustration by Giacomo Callo
Cover photograph by iStock
Typeset by J&M Typesetting

Printed and bound in the US by Lightning Source

National Library of Australia Cataloguing-in-Publication entry
Creator: Striano, Salvatore, author.
Title: Set me free : the story of how Shakespeare saved a life / by Salvatore Striano (translated from the Italian by Brigid Maher).
ISBN: 9781925498806 (paperback)
ISBN: 9781925626001 (ebook)
Subjects: Shakespeare, William, 1564–1616—Influence. Shakespeare, William, 1564–1616—Appreciation. Camorra—Fiction. Criminals—Italy—Naples—Fiction.
Other Creators/Contributors: Maher, Brigid, translator.

'Most welcome, bondage; for thou art a way,
I think, to liberty'

Posthumus Leonatus in *Cymbeline*
Act V, Scene IV

PROLOGUE

'Misery acquaints a man with strange bedfellows!'

Trinculo in *The Tempest*
Act II, Scene II

Now what?

Monica is the one who sees them coming. She is looking out the window.

What's going to happen to me? What lies ahead?

'Everybody out! Come out with your hands up!'

Where to from here? From this enormous waiting room full of people going back and forth?

I have just enough time to take my identity card out of its plastic cover, tear off the photo, and swallow the rest. Yes, swallow it. In Spain, if they catch you with false identity papers you get sentenced to several more years. Better to eat a bit of cellulose.

This place has such a familiar feeling to it. It's a place for waiting, where lives pass by quickly. I look around and I can almost hear the announcements: arrivals, departures, as though I'm waiting for the umpteenth train, the umpteenth escape.

I come out of the house with my hands up. From behind me I sense Monica's anguish. It's all over.

It seems like it might be the platform of a train station, but it's actually the reception area of a prison.

'Salvatore Striano, you're under arrest.'

So here I am, sitting and waiting to find out my destiny. Where will it take me? What land of troubles is it coming from, and what other darkness will it lead to?

What other evil?

PART ONE
THE JUNGLE

'Who dies, that bears not one spurn to their graves
Of their friends' gift?'

Apemantus in *Timon of Athens*
Act I, Scene II

1

'Time shall unfold what plighted cunning hides,
Who covert faults at last with shame derides.'

Cordelia in *King Lear*
Act I, Scene I

When you know trouble is brewing, and it finally comes, it's at once both a bad moment and a good moment.

This is true for everybody, and it was true when they came to get me. That was the end of my brief period as a fugitive. But it was also the end of a nightmare.

11 January 2000, Valdemoro Prison, Madrid. After I spent three years in hiding in Spain, they found me. It was probably a tip-off. But from who? I don't know, I don't want to think about it and, in a way, I don't care. I'm done with the Hotheads, done with gang life.

In truth, I'm done with a lot of things, now that I'm in prison. I'm done with the sky, which from today will be just a square of fresh air. I'm done being on the run; instead it'll be steps in the exercise yard. I'm done with my wife's laugh, which will become a forced smile across the table in the visiting room.

I think of my mother, who is sick. Will I be able to find out how she's doing, to get news of her? Maybe. As always, she'll be less worried knowing I'm in prison rather than out causing trouble and risking getting killed. But now that I'm in here I won't be able to go and visit her back in Italy…I start wondering whether it's worth trying to escape. I realise it's in my interests to serve out my sentence. I don't want to be on the run for the rest of my life. I go over the different possibilities and scenarios in my head, just to kill time, the only thing left worth killing.

'Do you speak Spanish?' The guard's voice rouses me from my thoughts.

I look up slowly—no need to jump to attention. I'm thinking, *Of course I speak Spanish, I've been in this country for three years, it's not like it's a difficult language.*

But I say, '*No comprendo*,' with an intentionally blank look.

The guard stares at me; he's not convinced.

'Follow me,' he says in Spanish, and off he goes.

I sit there motionless. No way I'm getting shafted by a little trick like that. I won't admit I speak Spanish, not for anything. I want an interpreter with me when they take me into one of these little white rooms. Someone from outside, who will see if they beat me or shove me around. Who will understand if they threaten me. I might be a criminal but I demand my rights. All of them.

The guard turns around and sees that I haven't followed him. He gives up.

'We'll get an interpreter,' he says, talking slowly because he has his doubts now, and is starting to think maybe I really don't understand Spanish.

The reception area is a bit like the lobby of the prison, the first gate you pass through once you lose your freedom. It's where they fingerprint you, take photos and give you clothes if the ones you have are no good, because it could be that when they picked you up you were wearing a hoodie with drawstrings. No drawstrings in prison: they're a weapon.

I huddle into my leather jacket. This place is full of draughts. It wouldn't even enter my head to hang myself, not with hoodie strings, not with anything. I'll serve my time with my head held high. So far the guards have been polite to me. They haven't beaten me or restrained me, they've let me smoke. It's a good sign. Maybe too good. What's the catch?

This big room, with its vaulted ceiling, is divided into lots of little rooms, each one closed off like a horse stable, and the grey and white walls also have a good deal of red on them. Blood that spurted from someone who was then taken away. I stare at one long stain, broken up by what could be scratch marks. I try to see a message in it, like you do with clouds. That's another thing I'm done with. Clouds.

They call my name and I throw my cigarette on the ground. The interpreter has arrived and it's a young woman. Her hair is in a ponytail and she looks too neat and clean for a place like this. She accompanies me into one of the 'stables', where there's a guard sitting at a desk, who will tell me how things work in here.

'You have the right to one phone call a day of ten minutes in length. To this end, you have the right to purchase a telephone card from the commissary. You have the right to one meeting a week with relatives and friends,' he begins, breaking off every so often for the interpreter to translate. 'You have the right to a four-hour conjugal visit from your wife or partner, in a bedroom made available for that purpose.' I'm keeping a blank face until she has translated each bit into Italian, to hide the fact that I can actually understand him, but it's hard not to give the game away when he says that. A bedroom?

'You are not allowed in your cell between 8 a.m. and 8 p.m.,' he goes on. 'You must spend these hours in the common room or outdoors.'

I can hardly wait for the girl to translate this piece of information so I can ask the obvious question bouncing around in my head.

'I can't stay in my cell all day, I get to use the phone and I have the right to make love to my wife. Sorry, guard, but are you sure I'm in jail?'

Maybe he can understand a bit of my Italian, or maybe he just picks up my tone of voice—the fact is, he almost smiles.

'I'm not your guard. Call me don Pedro,' is all he says, in a serious tone. 'Yes. You are in jail. Welcome to Valdemoro Prison.'

I get a sudden flash of inspiration. When I arrived, I saw some men in the corridor who weren't in uniform but weren't accompanied by guards, either.

'Does this mean that those men I saw outside weren't guards?' I ask.

'They're inmates, just like you,' he replies.

'And the guards?'

'Why the fixation on guards? There are no guards here.'

To understand why I leave the little stable feeling like I've won the lottery, you have to know what prison is like in Italy. I know all too well. My mother's been inside. So have most my friends back home in Naples, and so have I. The first time was when I was fourteen years old and sent to juvenile detention.

In Italy, you have to stay in your cell for the whole day, except for an hour and a half in the morning and an hour and a half in the afternoon, when they cram everybody into the exercise yard like a bunch of chickens in a coop. In Italy, you get to call your family from the prison phone once a week, or once a fortnight, but certainly not every day. And if they catch you with a mobile phone on your person they don't just rap you over the knuckles, they subject you to the Hard Prison Regime under Article 41b—all because you wanted to hear Mamma's voice. In Italy, only relatives have visiting rights and you can forget about conjugal visits: until you get out, your wife may as well be a widow.

But in Italy, your life is less at risk than here in Spain.

This is something I'll only come to understand later.

The guard taking me up the stairs looks like Zorro—tall, dark, thin, with a little black moustache. Suddenly he turns and takes me by the wrist.

'It's best if you take this off,' he says, tugging at my gold bracelet with 'New Millennium' engraved on it. The millennium is only eleven days old and I'm already in prison. That doesn't seem like a great start.

I stop, immediately on the alert. We're alone, having left the interpreter downstairs.

'This too,' the guard adds, pointing to the chain around my neck, also gold.

It had to happen sooner or later. This prison was too good to be true…I get ready for a fight. There's no way I'm letting him take my chain. It's got a locket with a photo of my father. He's only been dead a few months.

These bastards. The rage rises up from my stomach like acid.

But what can I do to defend myself? The guy's armed. Sure, I can shout. But they're all deafer here than in a nursing home.

'You get what I'm saying?' he presses me.

What's to get? You're trying to rob me. I'd like to tell him I understand perfectly, that this is my father's locket, that he's a bastard. But I'm pretending not to know Spanish, and if they realise I was lying about that I'll be in real trouble.

The guard shrugs.

'I'd take off your jewellery if I were you. It's not like in Italy. In here, you're on your own. And they'll end up stealing it off you.' He's speaking slowly, looking me right in the eye. 'You get it?'

So he was just warning me?

'*No comprendo*,' is all I say, trying to hide the relief in my voice. He wasn't trying to rob me, he was just trying to tell me there are some bad eggs in here.

Who'd have thought?

Zorro shrugs again and keeps heading up the stairs.

It seems like a million steps but it's just a few flights and then we arrive at a fork with an arrow. To the right: 'Units 1–5'. To the left: 'Units 6–10'. Two long corridors, lit just enough to look tragic, with arched ceilings, like an infinite series of tunnels with no way out.

We take a right. I'm not afraid, but in these tunnels there's a silence full of echoes that's making my head pound. To distract myself, I look at the drawings that break up the grey from time to time, evidently done by inmates. I stop in front of one: it's a view from above of a courtyard surrounded by huge walls. The perspective is dizzying, as though you're really up the top looking down. Black and brown birds are flying across the little square of sky in the foreground, their wings spread wide and their feet stretching down towards the ground. Each one holds in its claws a man's head, which hangs above the void.

It's a strange, ambiguous image. You can't tell if it's about freedom or fear. If these men have been rescued, or if they're prey.

Outside this big grey rectangle is the world, but the world is not necessarily a nice place. Everybody on the inside knows that.

'Are you coming?' I hear the guard's voice at the same time as I hear the sound of a gate opening. We've arrived at the end of the tunnel. I'm so struck by the drawing that I hurry through as though I'm heading to safety.

But beyond the gate is just more tunnel, with no end in sight.

The guard keeps talking but I'm no longer listening. I start thinking of the alleyways of the Quartieri Spagnoli, back in Naples. Some of them seem like tunnels, too, so narrow that it looks like the tops of the houses are touching. Suddenly I long for any place with light, colour, noise. In those alleys, though they're devoid of light, there's no shortage of noise and colour. The tunnel I'm walking down starts throbbing with the hum of motorbikes, like when the whole gang would take to the streets to show everyone that the Hotheads were fighting right alongside ordinary people. It resounds with the exploding tongue of fire coming from that one bazooka shot out to the sea the time we got our hands on enough weapons to destroy half the city. It fills with the soft rustle of money. And my friends' cries as the bullet arrives. Just like the bullet that, back home in Naples, has my name on it.

We pass through no less than four of these gates. At each one there's a sentry box made of bulletproof glass, surrounded by CCTV cameras, with a guard inside. A bright, clean little cage that looks like a hotel lobby. I'm starting to think these tunnels will never end, that I've been sentenced to walk up and down forever, like in a nightmare, my head pounding with memories. But then at the fifth sentry box, after the fifth gate, we stop.

'*Quién eres?*' the guard asks from behind the glass.

'*No habla español*,' Zorro informs him, explaining who I am.

They talk for a bit and I realise they're not going to put me in a cell on my own. It sounds like there will only be two of us. Could be worse.

Or at least that's what I think.

'Hey, Toc-toc! I mean…Michele! I'd forgotten you were in here too!'

While I wait until it's time to go into the cell that I've been assigned—they won't take you at just any hour of the day, you have to wait until 8 p.m., when everybody goes back in—I'm sitting in the common room of my unit, Unit 5. It's another big room—just for a change—full of men talking, wandering around, playing games. I'm keeping to myself. I don't yet know how things work here. It's not like the school canteen. If you sit at the wrong table in a prison, it can cost you your life.

That's when I see Toc-toc.

Michele is from Naples, like me, but that's where the similarity ends. He's a chubby, thickset, bald young fellow, so switched on that he earned himself the nickname Toc-toc, because you have to thump him on the back before he'll notice that you're talking to him, like knocking to see if anybody's home. Sometimes it's as though his brain is uninhabited.

But he's been in here three months, so he must have some

clue about the place.

'Hey, what's all this about phone calls, conjugal visits, a common room—is this even a prison?'

'Sasà, it's a jungle,' he says, shaking his head.

'But there aren't even any guards in here.' I gesture around the room. There are just a whole lot of ugly faces, including our own. You can spot the guards on a glassed-in upper level. They watch us from there, but we can do what we like down here. 'We're even allowed to wander up and down the corridors by ourselves,' I add.

'Yeah, sure, there are no guards.' But his tone is not happy in the least.

He's the slow one, not me, so I cotton on at once. Of course. I should have thought of it earlier. No guards means you have to sort everything out yourself. Once you've sorted it out, the guards arrive. But there's no guarantee they'll find you alive.

I look at the faces around the room again, and this time they look even uglier than before. And now it feels like they're all looking at me. The way you'd look at your prey.

'Come to the Italian table,' Toc-toc says, with the air of someone who knows the ropes.

Now let me be clear—Toc-toc has never known any ropes in all his life. He's inside because he got picked up with five hundred kilos of hashish—need I say more? He's one of those guys dealers get to deliver stuff, knowing it'll only last so long because he wasn't born smart and he's not about to become smart. Yet right now he's strutting around like he owns the place.

When I get to the table and say hello to everybody they're playing poker. Anyone not playing is following the game, so most of them barely look up, a couple give me a nod. I take the opportunity to study them carefully.

So this is why Toc-toc fancies himself some kind of emperor. He's with this lot. He thinks he's invincible. Some people wear a mask and some people wear their face. With the Italians Toc-toc wears his face, but with everyone else he wears a mask. He cloaks himself in other people's power.

I knew there were some big shots in prison in Spain, but actually finding yourself among them is a whole other thing. You could go a long way with the experience you racked up in here. I relax a little. If I'm with these guys, maybe I'll get through without any broken bones.

'Which cell are you in?' Toc-toc asks softly, so as not to disturb the others.

'Twenty-eight.'

One of the men watching the game spins around and stares at me.

'They've put you with the HIV guy.'

Put me with what? My blood runs cold. I'm sharing a cell with someone who has a contagious disease and the guards didn't even warn me? What if he infects me? What if he uses the threat of his blood to steal from me? What if he's crazy? Why was he in a cell on his own before? What happened to his last cellmate? A hundred scenarios run through my head and none of them end well.

'He won't tell you he's HIV-positive,' the guy adds. 'The guards put you in there on purpose, to see how you react.'

So much for 'There are no guards here' and 'Call me don Pedro'; so much for friendly warnings on the stairs. They are guards, and they're bastards just like all the others. That's real nice, putting you in with someone who's got HIV to see what kind of an inmate you're going to be. Are you the kind who can solve his problems on his own, or the kind who creates them? If you kick up a stink they target you and make sure your stay in prison is terrible. I'm going to have to manage this on my own without any nonsense.

I'll show them exactly what kind of inmate I am.

When 8 p.m. comes around I go into my cell and pretend everything is normal. My cellmate is already in there. He's Spanish, but he's so long and thin and white he looks like a Swedish asparagus. He's got the lower bunk on the right-hand wall. Next to the bed is the toilet and on the wall opposite the bunk bed there's a stone shelf to put some things on, and two little cupboards for our personal effects. That's it. We don't need anything else, since we only come in here to sleep.

The HIV guy responds to my greeting but doesn't say anything else. He's flicking through a magazine. I arrange my things in the cupboard in silence.

I climb onto the top bunk and make my bed with the prison sheets and blanket. Then I come back down. He's completely calm, he doesn't take any notice of me. But I know he's keeping an eye on me.

I'm not sure what to do. I don't want to cause a scene and I'm tired. I go to the toilet, then climb back up on my bed and stare at the ceiling. Maybe he'll say something now, tell me he's HIV-positive. I can't be the one to start because I'm pretending I don't speak Spanish, but he doesn't know that. He could say something. Surely he's going to finish that stupid magazine and say something.

Dinner arrives and there's still not a peep out of him. We eat in a silence that keeps getting heavier.

Does he know that I know?

I find myself lying back down staring at the ceiling, without having resolved the problem. That's it, I'm going to have to get down and face him.

I can't hear a sound coming from the bottom bunk. Maybe he's fallen asleep. What do you know—I'm going to have to wake him up to punch his lights out.

But maybe he thinks I'm asleep and that's why he's not talking to me.

Okay, I'm going to lean over. Yeah right, and what am I going to say? And in what language?

Stewing over all these alternatives, I end up falling asleep. And when I wake up the HIV guy is doing something really strange.

He's standing in front of the cupboard, naked from the waist up, and he's wrapping magazines around his chest, attaching them with sticky tape. He opens one, places it on his body, opens another and places it so that the edges overlap, then takes another one and he's back at the start—he's so skinny that three magazines go all the way around. Then he gets going on another layer.

The man's not just HIV-positive, he's crazy.

That's it, if I don't clear this up right away there's going to be trouble. I jump down from the bed. He turns and gives me a kind of smile, handing me the magazine he's holding.

'You want some?' he says in Spanish. 'I've got some spare, but you'll need to replace them.'

I'm on him in a flash. I spin him around and pin him against the wall. He's light and thin, and when he hits the wall some plaster falls into his hair. Looking frightened, his hair dusted with plaster, wrapped up in magazines like some kind of human sandwich, he's such a comical sight that I almost burst out laughing, but that feeling soon passes. He could probably kill me slowly.

'When were you going to tell me, eh?' I tighten my grip, even though I don't need to, because he's already immobilised. In fact, he's shrinking away from me, like he wants to drive himself into the wall. 'When were you going to tell me you're HIV-positive?'

2

'I'll fight, till from my bones my flesh be hack'd.
Give me my armour.'

Macbeth in *Macbeth*
Act V, Scene III

'You. Come with me. We're going to settle this at el Tigre.'

He spoke in Russian but I understood. The shadow cast across the wooden floor as he approached was about the size of a five-storey building. I don't even have to look up to know who it is. And I know who he's pissed off with.

He's Russian and everybody knows him. His name is Ivan.

My brain is whirring away like a computer in the few seconds I spend pretending to concentrate on the three kings I'm holding. I'm at the Italian table, so he can't do a thing. The Italians are the most powerful and the most respected group in here, and as long as we stick together nobody touches us. It's just like with the Hotheads back in Naples: if we went around in a group nothing could happen to us. The moment one of us stepped away, he got taken out.

Except that in Naples I could carry two guns everywhere I went.

It took me no time to work out the purpose of those gossip magazines my HIV-positive cellmate wrapped around himself. In here everybody wears magazines stuck one over the other like samurai armour. That way, when the time comes, before reaching your back the knife has to go through Prince Albert of Monaco, Belén Rodríguez, the Infanta of Spain on horse-back, and several other layers of gossip about the world's most beautiful people. If you're lucky, the blade only leaves a scratch. If you're unlucky, before knifing you they've taken you to 'el Tigre'—that's the bathroom, a place with no CCTV cameras—taken off all your magazines layers and broken all your bones.

Which brings us back to the great big Russian wardrobe standing by our table. I glance at the hand I'm holding my cards with. My thumbnail is white from clutching them too tight. I look up.

'Who have you got a problem with?' I ask. He spoke in Russian and I respond in Italian—we can understand each other just fine.

Antonio, sitting opposite me, nods imperceptibly. His eyes are saying, *Don't get up, tell him to fuck off, don't go with him. You're a damn fool*—scimunito!—*you gotta stay here! We can't get split up!* He's told me this a hundred times. He's an old Sicilian who's doing two life sentences; his extradition is taking a while because they don't have life sentences in Spain. They won't send you home if they think you'll be locked away forever back in Italy. But sooner or later the two governments always come to some kind of agreement. The Sicilian has taken a liking to me. He says that if my extradition goes through before his, he will miss me.

He'll be missing me even sooner than he thought if the Russian slits my throat in el Tigre.

Maybe I shouldn't have started smuggling in mobile phones.

I'd been in prison a few days when I took Toc-toc to one side and said, 'Let's go for a stroll.'

A stroll could help get my head around the current state of things. I'd already come to an agreement with my HIV cellmate. He turned out to be not such a bad sort after all. But I wasn't willing to share a cell with that sort of a chemical weapon, so I told him he had to cause a ruckus and get transferred somewhere else. He did. So that problem was solved without any nonsense.

Next I had to work out how to carve out a role for myself so that I could have a nice, quiet sentence and maybe put together a bit of money. This is not a prison, it's a jungle, and there's all kinds of stuff going on—drugs, gold…but it's not as though you can corrupt a guard with Monopoly money. What was going to be my business?

'I don't mind it in here, but making phone calls is a real pain in the arse…I've given up,' I ventured to Toc-toc.

'Hey, I can get you a phone, you know,' he replied, eager to please as always. My ears pricked up.

'What…so people sell them?'

He nodded. 'Two or three guys do. They get the guards to bring them in. We pay two million lire.'

It's classic street crime: the price doubles once you need to buy something illegal. Plus in here you've got the surcharge for the guard: a bribe of five hundred thousand lire (though, if you're lucky, you might make a little something with the exchange rate). A tray of lasagne? Five hundred thousand. A carton of smokes? Five hundred thousand. So two million, five hundred thousand is not that much. Why aren't there more mobile phones around?

'It hasn't really taken off,' says Toc-toc.

I can see that for myself.

'This will be my trade,' I declare.

A private mobile phone can come in handy for anyone. Sure, you're allowed one phone call a day, but what if you want to make two? What if you need to not only talk to family but also keep on top of your business dealings? If the guards catch you with a mobile phone it's two days in solitary, and that's not such a big deal.

There's a market to be made here, I thought.

'It's not easy to get them in,' Toc-toc warned me.

'Oh, isn't it?' I pretended to think about it.

'You need a guard,' he said earnestly, as though corrupting a guard was a difficult undertaking.

This is why Toc-toc will only ever be the errand boy, the one who waits in line to get his bosses coffee. But I'm no errand boy.

'They're not called guards, they're called don Pedro.' And I smiled, for the first time since I got here.

Actually, my guard is called don Juan. After a few days of scouting, I chose him.

'I wish they were all like the Italians,' he said. 'You guys are polite. You're people who know how to live life.' It's something I've heard from other guards, even other inmates.

'Listen, Juan. I need someone I can trust in here,' I explained.

'In what sense?'

'In all senses. For starters, I need someone to pick up my wife from the airport and bring her here.' Once a month Monica flies in from Naples to see me, and I don't like her going around on her own.

'You want me to be your driver?'

'I want you to do everything. Accompany my wife, leave her with me for a couple of extra hours, run some errands...I'll give you whatever you want.'

'You can't give me everything I want.'

'I'll give you four million a month.'

He gave a start. All the guards look like they've just dragged themselves down God knows what mountain to get here. For someone like don Juan, four million lire a month is a nice little nest egg to put aside for retirement.

'I'll ask no questions. I accept.'

From then on, in addition to those tasks, don Juan brings me five mobiles a month that I resell to other inmates. That way I can pay him and buy everything I need, like hash and a tray of cannelloni once in a while. Because, while prison in Spain might be more humane than in Italy, the food they give you is diabolical. All these miserable soups…I live on milk and biscuits, sardines and tinned food.

I hide the mobile phones in packets of cereal, or biscuits or sugar: I open them carefully with a blade, so you can't see the cut, I slide the phone in and I reseal it to look as good as new. If the guards see a box is still sealed they don't open it when they come to do a search.

When you're wandering about, though, you keep your phone in your pocket and wear earphones. That way if you come across a guard you start singing to yourself, so he doesn't realise you were moving your lips because you were talking on the phone. There's so much singing going on, the place is starting to look like a scene from a musical. After some time, there are quite a lot of phones in circulation, because, it doesn't take me long to become number one in business.

Except that the previous number one was this Russian guy.

I look my Sicilian tablemate in the eye, to let him know I've got the message. Then I move some of the prison banknotes, which we're using as chips.

'I raise you,' I say softly. Then I finally look at the Russian. I stand up.

What am I? I think to myself. *I'm basically the walking dead. I may as well take a risk while I'm still alive...*We all have to die sooner or later. Preferably later.

'Follow me,' I order him, as though I were a metre taller than him and not the other way around. The most important thing is not what you feel inside, but the confidence you convey. With bullies like the Russian, that confidence becomes even more important. And that's why I see a puzzled look on his face: nobody treats the Moscow Colossus like that. He's wondering: what weapon must I be hiding? Could I somehow have smuggled in a gun?

I walk ahead, signalling for him to follow me, and I head towards el Tigre. I sense his mass of flesh lumbering behind me. I feel like I'm about to throw up but I force it back down.

I have no weapon, not even a knife. I wasn't looking for trouble but I always manage to find it anyway. I know that as soon as we both cross the threshold into the bathroom, I'm a dead man. Not even industrial-strength disinfectants can eliminate the smell of blood and terror from el Tigre. It's a place with no cameras. A place with no escape.

This is the end, I think as I approach the door, which feels like the door to hell. A short-lived hell, hopefully, where it will all be over quickly. (Possibly to be followed by that other hell.)

But I refuse to let the fear show on my skin or in my eyes. I turn and nod for him to go in. I hold the door open.

'Please,' I say in a wry, ironic invitation. 'After you.'

He has the face of a blond bull. I raise my chin. The message I'm communicating is that I'm not afraid, but he ought to be. *Look at me, you great big Russian, I'm not frightened. I'm pissed off because you interrupted my poker game.*

I can hear the cogs of his brain ticking over, like mine were just a minute ago. But his cogs are slow. He can't get beyond two plus two, so right now he's thinking: *If this guy is so keen to get me into el Tigre, it's got to be a trap. He must have some way of killing me. Everybody knows these Italians are always one step ahead of the devil himself.* And speaking of Italians…

He looks behind him. Big mistake: my mates are wearing the kind of scowl that leaves little room for doubt. If he gets out of the bathroom alive and I don't, he'll be next.

Is it really in his best interest to hurt me?

I can see the moment the final cog turns. Two plus two equals four, and four equals 'it's not in my best interest'.

There's an instant when I'm on the edge between victory and disaster. Time stands still.

Then the Russian turns and leaves without a word, pushing past the Italians who have gathered.

I reckon I'll lock myself in the bathroom for five minutes all the same. At least until my legs stop shaking.

When I get to my third month of Spanish prison I realise I have a problem: I don't want to leave.

Since the episode with the Russian, no one has given me any

trouble. My phones are selling better than at a shopping centre, and the Italians are stronger than ever. This is in part because, let's be honest, in this dump, there's nobody to match us: there are many of us and we're rich, powerful and smart. Even the guys from ETA respect us.

The Europeans in this prison don't cut too fine a figure: the English are good at distilling moonshine but as dull as a Latin Mass; the Russians, who are supposed to be cluey con artists, are keeping their heads low after their chief meathead's pathetic showing...The worst are the Spaniards with long sentences who have jobs in here: they're a bunch of worthless informers, and after thirty years inside have at most three teeth apiece. We Italians, on the other hand, are well organised with codes and rules—basically the complete opposite of what we're like on the outside. We're the best smugglers, we're the best poker players, and our names are always in the papers. We're the aristocrats; the rest of the inmates come to us for everything. We even write their love letters.

We only have to rely on others for a few items. Drugs, for instance. The South Americans have the monopoly on cocaine: one guy in here sent five kilos of the stuff to the judge who convicted him, just to spite him. The Arabs deal in hash. For heroin, it's the Turks, but they only deal on the outside. Heroin has no place in here. It's a drug for losers. Soft drugs are the start of something messy, for sure, but they're not connected with so much drama. Heroin annihilates you, it extinguishes you, takes away your dignity, makes you unpresentable.

There's very little of it in circulation.

'I see you,' says the Little Prince, who has come to play poker at the Italian table. He's the only foreigner we'll accept because he sells drugs to us. He's under thirty, tall and elegant, with a long, dark face and an actor's good looks. He really does look like a desert prince and he is, in fact, rolling in money. He's crap at poker, though—any time he has a good hand he goes all red in the face. He loses twenty or thirty million lire a day and just laughs it off. His uncle provides petrol to the drug dealers back in his country, he owns all the service stations from Ceuta to Rabat, along the main trade route for hash.

You make a lot of useful friendships in prison.

'I fold,' I say, putting my cards down on the table. I've got to meet with don Juan, who will be handing over a bunch of mobile phones. This is strange. Tomorrow Monica is supposed to visit, and that would be an ideal time for the delivery. Usually I arrive in the visiting room with my bag of stuff—some food so she and I can eat lunch together, that sort of thing—and when don Juan comes to get me at the end of the visit he puts the phones in the bag. Then he pretends to search me, and that's that.

So why has he brought the delivery forward to today?

I bring Toc-toc along, who has become my official translator—I'm still pretending not to know Spanish. This way, once in a while, someone lets something slip in my presence. And in prison, information is gold.

'Here you go,' says don Juan, handing me a bag with six

mobile phones. He's looking at Toc-toc, puzzled—don Juan knows I speak his language, so he's wondering why I've brought my translator.

I take a quick look around. There are at least two CCTV cameras.

Why is this arsehole is trying to frame me? Did Monica not transfer his payment for this month?

I don't reach for the bag, and I give him a dirty look.

'Huh?' He furrows his brow. 'These are the ones you asked for.'

Toc-toc begins faithfully translating but I gesture to him to keep quiet. This little farce is getting on my nerves and I need to think fast.

'Come on, then. Hurry up, before someone comes,' don Juan urges me. He's starting to look around, too, acting all on edge. He really is trying to frame me. I knew it.

With a nod of the head I indicate that he should come with me to el Tigre. He hesitates, but follows. So does Toc-toc, but I tell him to wait for me outside.

'What's up?' don Juan asks, annoyed, as soon as the door closes. 'Are you pulling out of the business?'

I lay into him like a madman. He's so surprised he drops all the mobile phones, but I know his surprise will only last a moment.

'Don't move a muscle and I won't get out my knife,' I say, even though I don't have a knife. 'If you behave yourself maybe I won't even get angry. But you need to explain why you're trying to screw me over.'

'Me, screw you over?' he sounds astonished. Genuinely. 'Sasà, have you snorted more than what's good for you? Were the phones I brought you no good?'

'Oh, they were good. But why are you delivering these ones now instead of during my visiting time?' I tighten my grip around his neck.

'Well, because one of the other guards was asking some strange questions…I thought—'

'Sure! And what kind of strange questions do you think they're going to ask *me* when they see me picking up a bag of prohibited items? It'll be strange questions followed by solitary confinement, perhaps with fast-track extradition thrown in for good measure! Is that what you want? What have I ever done to you? Hasn't Monica given you this month's money?'

'Sasà, who did you think was going to see you? We were the only people in the corridor, apart from that idiot friend of yours.' He's getting worked up too now, and it seems genuine. Is it possible?

'It was you, me, Toc-toc and *two video cameras*, Juan. What kind of a fool do you take me for?'

He stares at me. I see the astonishment light up his eyes. Then realisation. And then, unexpectedly, amusement.

Don Juan bursts out laughing, pressed up against the bathroom wall.

'Sasà…let me go, come on,' he says, panting. I'm so surprised I actually do let him go. What's with the hysterics?

When he's had a chance to calm down, he says, 'Do you really…video cameras…Sasà, those things aren't recording!'

'They're not recording?' Now I'm the one who sounds like an idiot.

'The CCTV cameras in this place don't actually record anything. They're just there as a deterrent,' he explains. 'But I thought you knew that.'

'How was I supposed to know that? Nobody knows that.'

'Well then, don't you tell anyone.' He bends down to pick up the bag. 'And take these off my hands, because if we stay in here any longer we really will be in trouble.'

He shoves the gear towards me.

'Look after yourself, Sasà, and try to calm down,' he says as he leaves.

I'm left standing in the middle of the bathroom holding the bag, until Toc-toc sticks his head in.

'Sasà, all good? I saw the guard come out…'

I stare at his big, placid face; he's wearing the kind of worried look a mother has when her son hasn't come home. And suddenly it's the funniest thing I've ever seen.

I start to laugh, right there in that shitty bathroom. 'All good, Toc-toc.'

How embarrassing. Video cameras that don't record. Who'd have thought. I've said it before and I'll say it again: I really want to serve out my sentence here. I don't want to go back to Italy.

3

'This world to me is like a lasting storm
Whirring me from my friends.'

Marina in *Pericles*
Act IV, Scene I

'Ask for an appointment.'

Pierre has come up to me in the coffee queue in the common room. He's my French friend, and he's awaiting extradition, too. He's been sentenced to twenty years.

I don't ask what he's referring to. He's already more or less told me. Pierre doesn't want to go back to France to serve out his twenty years. He's going to escape from hospital—three of his friends are going to turn up and make sure he's handed over to them. He's offered me the chance to escape with him.

What else can I do? Three days ago I was called to the

sentry box and told my extradition papers had come through. I've got forty days before I'm taken back to Italy. My run of luck will be over. In Italy I'll have to stay in my cell the whole time with the guards breathing down my neck. In Spain, prison's not costing me a cent—I'm actually making a little bit of money— but Italian guards are harder to corrupt than Spanish ones. And there aren't as many jobs you can do, apart from dealing. No more business means no more money.

But above all, no more intimacy. I won't be able to make love to Monica anymore. I'll barely get to speak to her on the phone.

Nothing is going to happen in the next two weeks. They'll let me have one more meeting with Monica, which was already scheduled. And then they'll come to get me.

I look at Pierre and nod. The first chance I get I put my name down for a hospital visit the same day as him. They take us there in groups.

I'll go to the hospital with him and I'll escape.

What else can I do? I've fought so hard, and I've lost.

When they brought me the paperwork, months ago, I laid it out on the table in front of everybody. It was my arrest warrant, setting in motion the extradition process. I'd paid forty million lire to stop these documents coming, to have them get lost back in Italy for a few weeks. If the paperwork hadn't arrived within ninety days of my arrest, they'd have had to release me. But it had arrived, brought specially by car from Italy. Someone had snitched, letting them know what I was up to. Someone who knew me well. A friend, in other words. Some friend.

That was all I had to read, those papers. Everything was in there. Timelines, my rights. Maybe there would even be some way of not getting extradited.

I appealed every last detail of the ruling all the way to the highest level. I became a regular at the judge's office. It was kind of like a bet between us. I've never asked for freedom. I've only asked for my rights.

'Can you reopen the case?' I asked him. 'These papers show that the way in which I was convicted was illegal.'

'Are you aware that you were convicted not just once, but three times?'

'Yes, I know, but I wasn't present.'

'You should have been present.'

'I know.' My Spanish lawyer had already told me off. If I hadn't been on the run, if I'd turned up to my trial, I could have presented extenuating circumstances, defended myself. Instead they convicted me in absentia. 'But I wasn't there. Why can't a citizen defend himself, explain his position, demand his rights?'

'The Spanish legal system doesn't allow for a trial to take place in the absence of the defendant, that's true,' the judge admitted. He'd understood. He knew what I was getting at. This case could make legal history.

This was the first time a detainee had asked for his help in changing the law.

'They can't extradite you immediately,' he concluded. 'You can work your way through each of the legal stages, and that will take time.'

It did take time. Reading through all the legal document-ation became my speciality. I looked over other people's as well. I got really good at spotting all the loopholes in an Italian extradi-tion order. I helped out a number of inmates with life sentences, as well as people who were convicted in absentia like me.

We had our last meeting.

'The law has been passed,' the judge said. The world fell down around my ears.

According to the new law regulating the common European jurisdiction shared by Italy, France, Spain and Belgium, you can no longer question the validity of a sentence handed down in another country. You must simply return their criminals home. Italy has been on high alert since the Mafia assassinated Falcone and Borsellino, and in Spain there have been a number of ETA attacks. So they've decided that everybody must take back their own terrorists.

But I'm not a terrorist.

'I'm a European citizen and I want to serve my sentence here.'

'It's not possible.' The judge was sorry. Our adventure was at an end.

'But I'm happy here,' I protested, but without any hope. 'Back in Italy there's the Camorra, the Mafia...I don't want to go back to all that.'

'But it's the same in here. People get knifed and deal drugs… It's not as if we don't know about it.'

'I want to defend what I've got.'

It was futile. It's all very well to be a European citizen, but some are more European than others. I'm an Italian European and I have to take my country's justice.

I've lost.

So tomorrow, I'm out of here. I'll go to the hospital with Pierre and then I'm gone. On the run again, with all that fear and uncertainty. But I'm not going back to Italy.

In the yard a Neapolitan inmate approaches me. He was arrested in Spain and he hasn't been inside for long. He hasn't even brought me his paperwork to look at yet.

'I know who got you arrested.' He explains that his police files included transcriptions of phone taps in which an informer mentions my name. There's a guy in it saying, 'Last week I got Striano picked up.'

He can tell me who the traitor is.

I only think about it for a second.

'Don't tell me. I don't want to know,' I say, picking up my pace.

He comes after me.

'But I have to tell you,' he insists. 'It's someone close to you.'

One of the Hotheads, for sure. My curiosity is making me hesitate. There were five or six of them who could have been informers or traitors. The cops picked me up on 11 January and I know I was grassed on around Christmas time. I'd even made sure the guys had a special Christmas, I gave everybody watches…I know when the police came to get me they were tailing Monica's family. How did they know to do that?

I realise that whoever it is, they're close to Monica. The traitor is the same person who told the court that I was trying to arrange for my documents to get lost. And they could only have found that out from Monica.

The Neapolitan opens his mouth to speak.

But if he tells me who betrayed me, my only dream from now on will be to hunt that person down as soon as I get out of here. I'll want only revenge. And really, I want to leave all that poison behind. Otherwise, nothing good will ever happen to me.

Shit, Sasà. What good is ever going to happen to you? You're in prison.

But still…

'I don't want to know,' I say, pushing him back and moving away from him.

That night I can't sleep.

I'm thinking about the traitor, about tomorrow morning.

It's eating away at my stomach.

Tomorrow will involve a shootout, that much I know. It's not as though we can just walk out of a hospital, like visiting relatives do. I know Pierre's friends. I had a bit to do with them in Marbella one time when a reckless bunch of Italians stole a thousand kilos of hash. It was not a pleasant experience.

Somebody might get killed tomorrow. And I don't want to shoot anymore…I'm fine doing business and smuggling, but I'm done with gunfire.

I turn over and over in bed like a frittata. I can't get any sleep. I can already hear the guns, as loud as they are in Naples.

The next morning, when Pierre comes by on his way to his appointment, he looks at me in astonishment. I'm in my cell. I've cancelled my appointment.

I give him a wave.

'Good luck,' I mouth.

I feel both light and melancholy, as he stands tall and walks on.

But I'm standing tall, too. I don't want to get out of here only to go into hiding again, having to worry about who turned me in, or use brute force to regain everyone's respect. I want to be respected for who I am, not feared for what I can do.

That evening at dinner, Pierre is missing.

I glance across at the French table and my eyes meet those of a guy who knows for sure. The others are saying, 'He's been admitted for treatment.' There's no television, so no one knows about the attack at the hospital. But if Pierre's not back, either something went horribly wrong, or they pulled it off.

Later on, at nine, when we're already locked in our cells, we see the Special Unit from Madrid arrive. They search Pierre's cell and take all his papers.

From the other cells, applause begins. In unison, heartfelt. One of us has made it. There's some whistling, and the mood is one of general cheer, as though we've all flown out, carried by the birds, like in that drawing on the wall in the corridor. All the best, Pierre.

I put on my headphones with the volume turned up high, and flop down on the bed. For the first time since deciding not to go to the hospital I feel stupid. I don't want to hear that applause.

I'm exhausted. I haven't slept a wink in nearly forty-eight hours, but here I am turning over and over in bed once again. *You always miss out on the good stuff, Sasà, I think to myself. You always miss out on the applause. You've got to be in it to win it, otherwise this is what happens. You had the chance to be involved, you could have gone along with them, and instead here you are.*

That applause should have been for me, but I've missed out on it.

Next week Monica is coming. It will be our last visit. After that, they will take me back to Italy. Any day now.

The bedroom is the kind that would make you queasy if you had to sleep there. The colour of the walls is that bad. Maybe this is the Spaniards' idea of relaxation and good cheer. But I'm not complaining: at least it's four walls that are different from what I'm used to, and that's easy on the eyes.

Today, though, any kind of cheer seems impossible.

Monica hasn't arrived yet. I sit on the sofa opposite the bed and its two little bedside tables. The door to the bathroom is on my left. It's just like a hotel room, but without a wardrobe. And like we would in a hotel, we spend the day here: the visit is supposed to go for four hours, but thanks to don Juan, I always get eight. We talk, we eat lunch, we make love. Sometimes we even fall asleep in each other's arms. As though everything is normal, as though everything is just fine.

But this is the last time. After this, nothing will be fine.

Who knows if I'll see her again. Italian prisons are more dangerous than Spanish ones, even though they keep you under tighter control. The common areas are enough to make you sick. You spend the whole day in your cell and the sensory deprivation dulls your senses—your eyesight and your hearing suffer. The guards don't talk to you, and there's no human contact, apart from the contact you get with criminals who have never stopped offending for a moment and aren't about to stop just because they're in prison.

They'll drag me back into that world. A world I thought I was done with. I've studied my case carefully and I know I have to try to cut down my sentence. Fourteen years minus a year and a half served in Spain minus preventive detention…That still leaves eleven years. It's a long time.

Will Monica wait for me? Would I wait for her? Of course I would.

No, I wouldn't. How could I go more than a decade without touching another woman? I wouldn't have the strength to stay away from that kind of temptation for seven or eight years.

I could ask don Juan to allow her come again tomorrow. To get her to come every day until they send me back to Italy. But then we wouldn't be making love. We'd be violating each other just to spite the people who screwed me over.

The last time I saw the judge I protested from the bottom of my heart: 'We went to church and swore before God that we would stay together for better and for worse. Nobody has the right to separate us.' I'm not one to beg, though I got damn close to begging him. But it was all in vain.

Monica enters and sees at once the state I'm in.

'Don't cry,' she murmurs as she sits down next to me.

'What am I supposed to do? It's all over.' I'm trying to hold back the tears but I know I won't last long.

'We'll see each other more often,' she says, taking my hand. I realise she's not despairing as I am. I look at her and I don't see sadness comparable to mine. Is it possible she doesn't mind that she'll no longer be able to make love to me for who knows how long?

'You'll see me in the same way you see animals in a cage,' I growl. That's exactly how I feel: like an animal that's been cornered. I tear my hand from hers.

'That's the way things are. There's nothing we can do about it.' She's raised her voice now, too.

'You don't even give a damn, do you? You have your freedom either way!' I get to my feet and turn my back on her. 'I'm the one losing everything. Intimacy, communication. Everything!'

If she feels like going off with some other guy tomorrow, she can.

This is not a pleasant thought.

'You can go off with another man any time, but where can I go?'

'I don't want to go off with anybody! What do you take me for? Show some respect!'

This time I can hear she has a lump in her throat, and I turn around.

'I'm not the one who got us into this,' she says softly.

If I look deep into her eyes I can see our whole life together. The day we met, the first time we made love, our scooter rides, the evenings back at my mother's place, cutting cocaine. She and my mother side by side on our little balcony, hoping I'd come home alive after the umpteenth day of the turf war. The ring I put on her finger and the chain we wear around our necks for all the mistakes we've made. Together.

I open my arms and she runs to me. We stay like that, tears running down our cheeks, through our hair, for ages, maybe for the whole eight hours, I don't know. I lose all sense of time. We don't even make love. Eventually I fall asleep, exhausted from having slept so little these past few days.

My dream is a kind of muddled blend of fairytales. The faces of people making fun of me, threatening me. 'You're ours,' they're saying. 'You're part of our story and you can't get out.'

Fairytales have always frightened me and now I know why. In prison I came to understand the meaning of them. They were reality—my reality. Lampwick and the evil puppet-master from *Pinocchio*, the big bad wolf, selfish giants—I've met them all in here. Except that when I was little I was fine hearing about them because I knew there'd be a happy ending.

There's no happy ending in here.

o

The guards arrive at six.

I already said goodbye to everyone I needed to last night.

I'm leaving, but I'm defeated. The match is over and I've lost.

As I walk through the prison I keep my eyes down. I don't even want to look around. No one whistles, no one claps. I'd be happy to hear anything but I hear nothing. Maybe some of them are saying goodbye, but it's complete silence in my head. I'm no longer here. I've left. I don't belong here anymore. It makes me mad that this place has made me feel sorry to leave it. For a moment they actually managed to institutionalise me. I should be able to think: it's best to move on to the next port of call, keep things moving. But my every thought just falls into nothingness.

The men who have come from Italy to collect me—a six-metre tall guy from Bari and his lanky offsider—put me in a car with a Spanish policeman at the wheel.

I already know that in Rome my own personal red carpet, complete with photographers, will be waiting for me. Let's go see that guy they extradited, the gangster, the dangerous Camorrista...the newspapers label you, and that's what you are known as when you're on the inside, too.

I can just feel it: my life ends here, on the other side of that invisible border in the sky, between Spain and Italy. A long living death awaits me now. Who knows if I'll get out and how?

INTERMEZZO

Let's just hope we make it to prison. All we need now is for the plane to crash.

This plane full of people who watched me climb on board in handcuffs the way you'd watch a trained monkey at the circus. These people who don't know anything.

They see something ugly, a man under police guard, a criminal, but they don't know what happened, they don't know anything about me. They don't know that sometimes, before you can judge, you have to understand. And that it's hard to understand, it's the hardest thing of all.

On the streets I learned that you should always hold your head high. But sometimes, you must do the opposite. When you live a life of crime it doesn't pay to look people in the eye—you might stare at the wrong guy. He'll make a mental note of it and a few years later, even if you've turned over a new leaf, he'll recognise you. I might run into these people from the flight in several years' time, after I've been released. If I look directly at them now, if I smile and look them in the eye, maybe they'll remember me. And I don't want them to remember who I am just this moment.

I'm someone who lost the match. I'm defeated.

People on the outside, the ones who grassed on me, will no longer be afraid of me. I won't even be able to make phone calls anymore. I'll have no power at all.

I almost don't care. I never wanted to be feared by that kind of scum. I would have liked a bit of respect. But in the end, respect is a word that floats off on the wind.

I met someone who wanted to tell me the name of an informer who was close to me. I've had mates who managed to keep out of prison and would say one thing to me on the phone but then go and do the opposite. And when I think that they were all people I'd helped out in one way or another—I'd fed them, cared for them, given them a place to sleep—I realise just what a piece of shit this life I've created for myself really is.

The giant from Bari, in the seat next to me, gives me a puzzled look.

'What, you're talking to yourself now, are you?'

'Yeah. That way you won't get bored.'

PART TWO

WHAT GOES AROUND COMES AROUND

'He jests at scars that never felt a wound.'

Romeo in *Romeo and Juliet*
Act II, Scene II

4

'The worst is not
So long as we can say "This is the worst."'

Edgar in *King Lear*
Act IV, Scene I

The cell windows face the yard, so we hear them arrive a little before six in the morning. We wake up immediately—you sleep lightly in prison. Their steps are rapid and rhythmic. It's a ministerial search. They've surrounded the building.

Here we go, I think. I've only been in Rebibbia Prison three weeks and I'm already in trouble.

We get out of bed and each hide what we need to hide: the little bit of hash your wife brought you, the coke you got from the guard. I don't have anything to hide because I smoked my last joint the night before. In any case, this isn't a routine inspection, one of those internal inspections they do after visiting day to check that no prohibited 'gifts' have slipped through. This is a search ordered by the ministry, which the Rebibbia guards weren't even told about, to make sure we prisoners didn't get wind of it.

This time they're looking for something. And I know what it is. And I'm afraid.

'Out! Wake up! All out!' The prison guards open the cell doors. They drag us out of bed and march us into the yard. From downstairs, their colleagues are keeping a close eye on the windows. That way, they'll know which cell it's from if something prohibited flies out, like hash or cocaine or knives.

Or mobile phones.

Standing out in the yard in a T-shirt and underpants like everybody else, it's not the fact that it's six in the morning that makes me feel the cold. It's the fact that I'm at risk of Article 41b of the Prison Act, the toughest and most restrictive kind of prison regime there is.

Because, even though I don't have a mobile phone, the four Camorristi I share a cell with do.

I knew it. I knew it would end this way.

Calm down, Sasà, I tell myself. *You've never used that phone. They can't do anything to you.*

They can do whatever they like to me, I reply.

When I first arrived in Rebibbia, my cellmates told me straightaway that they had a prohibited phone, which they kept in the Albanians' cell. They'd go to that cell every evening to eat and, over a glass of wine and a bowl of spaghetti, each one of them would take turns to slip into the bathroom and make his calls—to his wife, to keep on top of blackmail, threats, extortion, whatever business he conducted on the outside.

The inmates figured this would be enough to allay suspicion. Yeah, right. I told them this was not a smart move. I hardly ever visited the Albanians' cell. Instead I would go and socialise in another cell full of Neapolitans.

But don't you think the guards might occasionally wonder why a bunch of Italians are always going over to eat with these Albanians, invariably skint and not even our fellow countrymen? Doesn't that look a bit odd? Won't they start to think something fishy is going on? If I was able to spot it when I'd only been here five minutes, why wouldn't they arrive at the same conclusion?

Well, you bet they arrived at that conclusion. The guards have devices for detecting electromagnetic waves. I've seen them. They use them to hunt down mobile phones.

If they find a phone with the Albanians and work out that it belongs to my cellmates, they'll all end up on the 41b Hard Prison Regime. And I'll join them, because I'm living in the same four walls.

Right from the beginning I said, 'I'm not going anywhere near that thing.' This isn't Spain. Over here you're in massive trouble if you get caught with a prohibited phone.

So here we are.

A feeling of despair and humiliation runs along my skin like the cool dawn air. We've been kept out here in the cold in our underpants, stripped of our dignity. They won't believe me. They'll throw me in with the guilty criminals. I won't get to see Monica ever again. I won't get to see anyone. That's Hard Prison. And yet I didn't do anything…

But it's always been like that. That's how it was in the Quartieri, and back when I was a kid. Even if you haven't done anything—you're in the game so you've got to play, and sooner or later you'll lose.

One at a time, the guards start calling prisoners' names. They each drag themselves back inside and the yard gradually empties. Even the Albanians get called back in.

We five are the only ones left standing in the yard, and there's no longer any doubt. I have very little hope that they didn't find it.

How long has it been since they woke us up? I'm not wearing my watch but it must have been at least an hour. They call in the other four one at a time.

I'm left alone in a yard full of guards. I don't know if I've ever felt this frightened or powerless, not even when I found myself on the ground looking up into the barrel of a gun.

I almost feel relieved when they call me in. I'm really cold, and I was practically putting down roots in that yard. As I follow the guards I hold my head high and square my shoulders, faking a cocky swagger. My dignity is important to me.

Sitting behind the desk in the office, is a menacing-looking man I've never seen before.

'Are you Salvatore Striano?'

'Yes.'

'We've found an unauthorised communication device.'

One. In the entire G12 section of Rebibbia prison they've found just one 'device'. It's ours, of course.

I'd like to reply, 'You don't say,' but I bite my tongue. I try to look astonished but unconcerned.

'What, in my cell?'

He stares at me as if to say 'what a stupid question'.

'Like anyone would keep it in their own cell,' he says sarcastically.

'But if you didn't find it in my cell, why are you bringing me out for a stroll at six o'clock in the morning? And why are you treating me like a criminal? I thought I was in a state of divine grace.' Without a moment's hesitation I match his sarcasm with my own harsh tone.

Maybe something in my voice makes him hesitate. He starts to suspect that maybe I really don't know anything. But he doesn't want to believe me.

'Striano, you'd better be telling me the truth.' *Otherwise I'm gonna kick your arse*, his eyes imply. 'Take him down.'

'Down' means solitary confinement, and I'm sure it's gone exactly the same way for my cellmates.

Damn them, I think. I must've told them a hundred times these past three weeks that it was going to end badly. And they kept saying, 'We need to maintain our networks on the outside.' You see, even if you're locked up in an Italian prison, you can keep up your life of crime if you want. So much for rehabilitation.

In Spain, if someone had got me into this much trouble I'd have put him through a pretty nasty fifteen minutes or so. Sure, there are four of them and only one of me. But I managed worse when I was in the Hotheads. Ten against one, even, and all armed to the teeth.

I think back on those times as I sit in this minuscule, silent cell and they replay like scenes from an old film. Something really distant, happening to someone else, or perhaps a dream. I don't have any other film to project onto these white walls, or on the ceiling when I'm lying back on the marble slab that is my bed. In solitary, there's nothing to do but think, and nothing to think but bad thoughts.

Whenever the guard feels like it, he gives me a cigarette. There's no explanation provided. Let's just hope they're checking the call logs and realise I've got nothing to do with any of this. Let's hope those Albanian bastards didn't say that the phone belonged to the guys in cell 12 because then we'll all end up in here. Let's hope I don't end up with the bad-arse inspector who, even though he knows I'm not involved, punishes me anyway for not grassing on the others.

It's been only three weeks and I've already got myself into trouble, as my mother would put it. But I just wound up in this situation. It's not my fault. I'm answering back in my own head, thinking these thoughts both in my own voice and in my mother's scolding voice.

Some people go crazy when they're put in solitary. As for me, I'd actually be quite content with my own company, but my anxiety over that mobile phone is eating away at me. I can't stop thinking about the nightmare of the 41b regime that might be looming.

Then the guards come down. They take me back to the office. Our section inspector is there along with the commander who made fun of me the last time. When was that? Maybe four days ago, but who knows. It feels like four months.

As soon as he sees me come in, the commander stands up and stretches out his hand.

'Sorry about these last few days, Striano,' he says. 'But unfortunately we had to check the phone logs to see who'd used the thing. It's a nasty business.'

'I didn't do anything.' I shake his hand. I want him to acknowledge that I'm innocent. He nods.

'It's true. But your attitude, your *omertà*, this refusal to cooperate with us, is not in keeping with the policy of this penitentiary. It's holding you back from being involved in rehabilitation treatment.'

My eyes widen. 'You're telling me, just three weeks in, that I need to be on good behaviour? Why? What's happened? Can you at least tell me that?' I'm getting hot under the collar. Do they expect us prisoners to do their work for them now?

'You knew your cellmates had a prohibited mobile phone and you didn't say anything.'

'Do you really think we tell each other everything?'

'No, I'm quite sure that you keep things from one another. But I'm also quite sure that you knew that there had to be a reason why your friends went to eat with the Albanians every night.'

'Well okay, I suspected something, just like you suspected it. So what? That just shows that we're all as smart as each other.' I'm running out of patience. This is not a serious conversation, it's like something out of a street-side puppet theatre—each one of us is just playing their part, going through the motions. I might be in prison, but I haven't got time for this kind of farce.

'All right, you can go back to your cell,' the commander sighs. He got my drift pretty quickly: he'd been hoping to get some information, but he sure won't be getting any out of me.

'I'm not going back to my cell.'

'What do you mean you're not going back to your cell? What do you want? Do you think we're going to release you on good behaviour?'

'No.' *You're really not funny, commander*, I think. *You're not the one who has to do eleven years in here without falling into any more traps like the one I've just managed to make my way out of.* 'You have to do me a favour and take me back down into solitary confinement.'

He exchanges a glance with the inspector as if to say, 'Oh boy, we left him down there too long and he's gone nuts.'

'Why? Do you like it there?'

'I do,' I reply. 'There I'm alone. I can only get into trouble if I choose to, and I pay the consequences for my own behaviour and nobody else's. I'd like to be able to rest easy, thank you very much.'

I say all this pretty bluntly, maybe too bluntly, because the commander's face turns hard.

'Now you're going overboard,' he warns me.

But I stick to my guns: 'No, I'm not going overboard. You put me back in solitary confinement, and then when a private cell becomes available you put me in there. Otherwise, I'll serve my whole sentence down in solitary. It's all the same to me. The food trolley comes by either way, and that's all I need.'

He looks me in the eye. It's a proper staring contest.

'Take him back down,' he says in the end.

A couple of days later the brigadier comes and lets me out.

'One of the workers has been released,' he says. The workers, the ones who take care of cleaning and other services within the prison, get private cells because they have to wake up at five in the morning. 'You're going into number 16.'

I go into my private cell feeling like I've won a little war. I don't want to have to rely on others. I never have—not even on the streets of the Quartieri—and I never will.

Having a cell to myself means I'm automatically able to avoid a lot of risks. But I can't avoid them all. There's one small problem: I'm Sasà from the Hotheads, and here, they all know it. My return was in the newspapers the day after I arrived from Spain. Salvatore Striano, member of the Neapolitan gang the Hotheads, who set up a dangerous drug trafficking ring in Spain...I've been branded.

But someone like me is a bit of a foreign body in a prison like this, which is crawling with members of the Neapolitan

Camorra. See, although I was also a criminal, I spent years fighting *against* the Camorra. All the inmates know who I am. Some show me respect, because no one has ever been sure whether the Hotheads, that invincible brotherhood, was made up of ten, a thousand, or five hundred thousand men, so who knows how many there might be in this prison, ready to leap to my defence. But of course there are others who want to challenge me: I took on the Camorra clans of Naples, and now they want to take me on.

I need a guard.

Not to bring me hash: Monica does that when she comes to visit—she passes it to me with her tongue when she kisses me. What I need now is different: protection, information. I need to work out where I stand, and find out who the traitorous *infami* are. I'm not part of the Camorra loop and I'm very isolated in here. But it's not easy with the guards. If you talk too much you're dangerous, because you might talk. If you say nothing you're dangerous, too, because that's *omertà*—you must be covering for someone. You can't win.

Luckily, I've never been in a place where I haven't been able to win over a guard in a few hours. It just takes a few more days in Rebibbia than it did in Spain. They start to soften up when they learn that I can speak Spanish and they can call on me to translate when a South American prisoner comes in. Then they learn that I'm a no-nonsense guy who minds his own business. They're real psychologists, these guys. They spend more time with us than with their wives and they end up tuning in to the way we think, the way we feel.

In Rebibbia my guard is called Gaetano. He approached me one afternoon in the yard and struck up a conversation. He's from Naples, like me, and he does me the favour of calling my family to see if everything is okay, because I'm only allowed to use the phone every so often and that's not enough. Once in a while he brings in a bottle of wine for me, something I need, and he keeps me up to date with what's going on. He's a lot cheaper than don Juan. On the other hand, he talks a whole lot more—he's developed the habit of telling me his whole life story, one episode after another. He's got problems with his brother, who has got mixed up with the wrong crowd, so from time to time he asks me for advice. It's pretty funny to think I've become a kind of special consultant on the criminal underworld.

I don't always feel like listening to Gaetano. Especially when he comes by at eleven o'clock at night. And especially when I'm in a bad mood, like tonight.

Monica was here yesterday, and she told me that my mother couldn't come and see me this time, either. She hasn't visited once since I've been in prison in Italy. I haven't seen her since the days when I was in hiding in Spain, before I got arrested. I've spoken to her, but it's not the same as having her here. I have to see her to know if she's doing all right. 'She'll come next week,' Monica repeats, but I know she's not telling the truth. Only one thing would stop my warrior mother from coming to see me, and I'm scared I know what it is.

Gaetano parks himself in front of the door of my cell where

I've been minding my own business. He looks inside and asks, 'What are you thinking about? Love?'

'Love? In prison?' I ask bitterly. 'That stuff's for the rest of you.' Those of you who are free, is what I mean. Those of you who don't have to look at your loved ones through a grille.

'Not me.'

That's right, I'd forgotten Gaetano's also got problems with his wife.

'My commiserations,' I say sullenly. *Get out of here*, I think. *It's not a good night for this.*

'What's wrong? Am I bothering you?'

I look up, struck by his wounded tone. He has the sweet, round face of a character in a film, who always dies in the second scene. Poor guy.

'No, you're not bothering me,' I say.

And off he goes. Talking about his wife. The warden. The prison. And after a while I start talking, too. Not about prison but about Naples, about the sea—I'm trying to drag him out of this place, at least mentally, just like I wish I could do for myself.

'I could see right from the early days that you were different from the others,' he says at the end of what seems like a long confession.

I'm different? I mean, I've always known that. But I'm different in the sense that I'm maladjusted, a hothead. Even in here I refuse to let anyone tell me what to do, where to go, what to think—whether it's guards or prisoners. I'm a rebel. There's only one person who has always been able to tell me what to do.

Mamma. The one time she came to see me in Spain she made me swear: 'Fight it. You've got to fight not to be sent back to Italy.'

I fought and I lost. *I came back to Italy, Mamma. I disobeyed you, but it's not my fault. I hoped I'd at least see you again. But you won't come. You won't come...*

'I can still imagine her out on the balcony waiting for me,' I say to Gaetano, following my train of thought rather than the conversation. I haven't spoken about her in months.

That's when I realise something's not right.

Gaetano never got past fifth grade, but he's a fine psychologist—like I said, all the guards are. Gaetano wouldn't even be able to explain how he did it, but somehow he'd got our little chat to head in that direction.

It's almost three in the morning, the darkest time of night. I realise that Gaetano has been quiet for a while. I shake myself out of my thoughts and turn to him; in the shadows I meet the whites of his eyes. Suddenly I realise why he ended up at my cell tonight. I want to be wrong but I'm not.

'Why did you come here?' I ask quietly.

'Oh, I just felt like talking.'

'Why did you come here?' I repeat, and this time my tone is menacing. I might be locked in a cell but the voice coming out of me is that of someone who could grab Gaetano by his neck and squeeze until it broke.

'Sasà,' he sighs. His tone is one of surrender, and my name sounds like the toll of a funeral bell. 'I didn't want you to find out over the phone. Your mother's dead.'

5

'You may my glories and my state depose,
But not my griefs; still am I king of those.'

Richard in *King Richard II*
Act IV, Scene I

'Whoa, you kicked the ball right into my face!' the goalkeeper roars. My penalty kick almost cost him an ear.

'Well, why didn't you move?' I shout back resolutely.

'Because I've got to stop the ball!'

'Go on, then, stop it. Play!' I give him a fuck-off gesture, which he returns.

I'm playing football like it's war. I'm kicking penalties not to score goals but to hurt.

To hurt the way I'm hurting.

We're at the height of the regional tournament between

Campania, Sicily, Calabria, Puglia and Lazio. Lombardy and Friuli-Venezia Giulia don't have enough inmates to form a team, oddly enough. Today's the big match—Sicily versus Campania. It's a proper Mafia derby.

'What's up with you?' asks Antonio, who's playing defence. He puts a hand on my shoulder but I shrug it off angrily.

'Nothing's up with me. I'm playing football, aren't I?' I'm basically telling him to fuck off, too. 'What is this—a football match or a knitting circle?'

What can you do? Everything's going badly today.

On the other side of the field, the Sicilian side, they've taken advantage of this argument to bench Leonardo. Poor guy. He gets on well with the guards, does everything he's told, is always on his best behaviour and was supposed to be going to Mass today but instead was forced to play football. And now they've sent him off first thing. Just to spite him.

I see him mournfully dragging himself to the edge of the field. He's missed out on going to Mass but he can't go back into his cell until the exercise hour is over. He's looking away so nobody can see that he's close to tears, but I notice. So does the Sicilian who sent him off. He goes after Leonardo.

'What, you're crying now? Stop crying, or you'll spoil our fun!'

Nope, that's it.

'Sasà, where are you going?'

Where am I going? To punch that bastard's face in.

'Leave him alone.'

The Sicilian looks at me in astonishment. He hasn't been inside for long so he doesn't know who he's dealing with.

'What do you want?'

'I want you to leave him alone,' I repeat, in case it wasn't clear the first time.

'Or else?'

That's it. I'm going to kill him, I suddenly realise. I'm so full of rage and frustration that if I start beating him up I will actually kill him. I won't be able to stop myself. I can't stand people like that, who pick on the weak. Sure, Leonardo's crap at football, but this guy has no right to do this.

I clench my fists. My body is tense, like a tightly strung bow made entirely of nerves. For days now, weeks, I've been building up tension; my rage keeps growing, but I haven't found any release, not even through rough play on the football field. Out on the field you run, but it's not enough. You don't use up your strength, you don't vent your emotions. I'm ready to explode.

The Sicilian's teammates quickly surround him and whisk him away. They're worried. They know the way I've been lately and if there's trouble, who knows how long we'll be banned from playing. Here in Rebibbia, it's unlikely someone will beat you up. Nothing ever happens among inmates, partly because of the risk of a tougher sentence, and partly because the mentality in Italy is that once you're in prison, the war is over. You enter prison to serve time, not to carry on wars: they used to do that in the seventies, but not anymore.

The Sicilian lets his friends take him away, and they explain to him who I am and why it's not a good idea to make me angry. I hear the other guys' voices telling me to let it go, but it's as though they're coming to me through a red fog.

I shove them away violently and go and sit in a corner of the yard.

I hate everybody. It's been two weeks since my mother died and it's been two weeks since I slept.

I talk to her. She might be dead but she's certainly not gone.

'You're crying. *Now* you're crying?' she reproaches me bitterly.

'So what if I am? Aren't I even allowed to cry?'

'You should've thought of that earlier! Before you left me all on my own!'

'You're the one who told me not to come back to Italy. You made me swear!'

'Because if you had come back they'd have killed you! But who got you into all that trouble? Was it me?'

'I got into it by myself, so why don't you just leave me there? At least leave me in peace!'

'Get up off your arse. You're a shit of a man, that's what you are!'

'Well, if I'm a shit of a man it must be because you made me that way!'

It's like that all day and all night. My mother has become my worst enemy. Towards dawn I plunge into an exhausted sleep, confused, agitated, and when I wake up and see her photo on the wall I'm consumed by rage and the whole thing starts over again. At one point I thought about tearing it into confetti, but then I couldn't do it. My head is full of hatred for everybody and full of painful tears that don't know how to get out.

Now I'm doing the exact opposite of what she taught me. I'm doing whatever I feel like. I've reverted to being a *guappo*, a swaggering criminal, like when things were at their very worst on the streets of the Quartieri. I don't greet anybody in the corridors, I keep to myself, with my eyes to the ground. I've started running in the yard, as though it's possible to escape this thing that's inside me. I play football violently, spitting out swearwords.

'Has something happened?' the guys keep asking, but they don't get that I'm still in this state because of my mother's death.

'Why are you asking? Why does something have to have happened?' I always answer angrily.

I'm being de-habilitated. I'm once again the guy that used to say to the local Camorra boss, 'You want watches? Go and steal them yourself then.' The guy who got condemned to death because he refused to be intimidated. I've sent Monica away twice. I don't even want to see her. She arrived in Rome from Naples with a package of freshly washed things for me, and I didn't go down to meet her. They brought up the package and I sent that back, too.

Why didn't you tell me you were so sick? I'd have escaped, I'd have run away and come to see you. Why didn't anyone tell me you were on the way out, that I would never see you again?

I don't give a damn about good relationships, good manners,

or anything in this shitty life anymore. I don't care that if I keep this up I'm going to fall apart. If I was the kind of person to kill myself, perhaps I'd kill myself, but taking my own life is the very last thing on my mind. Finding a way to kill me has always been other people's concern; mine has been finding a way to stay alive. This was my mother's problem, too.

See, Mamma? You're free of problems now. You're free of me. Are you happy?

After two weeks I give up.

In the morning I go to the infirmary.

'Give me some drops.'

'The doctor has to prescribe them.'

I go to the doctor.

'The psychiatrist has to prescribe them.'

I go to the psychiatrist, ready to smash the place up.

'Give me some drops.'

'Why do you believe you need medication? Are you troubled?'

'Of course I'm troubled!' I explode. 'You've got no idea what you're talking about!'

'Can we talk about it? What's the problem?'

'You already know the problems a prisoner has,' I say through clenched teeth. I don't want to talk to him about my mother. 'This shitty place, the never-ending night, the thought of my wife who might be cheating on me, I can't take it anymore, you have to give me some drops!' I get agitated, I shout, I don't even know what I'm saying. I obsessively repeat the same thing: give me the drops, give me the drops. I already know that you give them out to everybody, that hundreds of us are on sedatives, why can't I be, too? Why should I have to be stronger than everyone else, better than everyone else? Give me some fucking drops, so I can calm down and get this war out of my head.

I finally get through to the doctors. They prescribe the damn drops: forty in the morning, forty in the afternoon and forty before bed. One hundred and twenty drops a day, a dose fit for a wild horse. Then, just to be on the safe side, there's this South American kid who doesn't drink, and I get him to give me half a litre of wine in the morning and another half in the evening. I'm not allowed wine because I'm on medication. He buys it for me, two cartons of wine for two euros, and I give him two packets of cigarettes in exchange, which are worth twice as much. So I'm sorted.

In the morning, forty drops and a quarter-litre of wine, in the afternoon forty drops and another quarter-litre of wine, and in the evening forty drops and half a litre of wine. A litre of wine plus the drops and I'm laughing to myself in my cell like a halfwit. I no longer care that my mother died, I no longer care about anything. The mix of drops and alcohol eliminates all feeling—pain, fear—and makes me contemptuous, rude, indifferent. The cruellest hour is when I first wake up in the morning, I open my eyes and I'm dazed but sober, I see her things, her photo, and I'm assailed once more by that need to cry tears that won't come, the rage rises within me, the voices in my head start up again. I grab my bottle of drops and carton of wine.

And then everything's fine. It's the only way. It's all over, apart from this shitty living death that continues to drag on.

Cosimo turns up unexpectedly one afternoon. He's doing a life sentence. They told me as soon as I arrived that he's on good terms with the guards, but he's no *infame*; it's in the interests of helping the other prisoners, not to snitch. He's in charge of activities and courses. When I was still doing all right he asked me to write the match reports after every game. I've given that up now and haven't talked to him for a while. Or to anyone, for that matter.

I can hear him arriving from a long way away because he's greeting people loudly as he walks along the corridor. If he's out of his cell today it must be because he needs to organise one of his activities. But he's usually very discreet, so why is he making all this racket?

It's like he wants to announce his arrival to me. In fact, a short time later he stops at the door of my cell. He's never come to see me before. He leans on the little barred window and asks, 'Everything okay, Sasà?'

'Yeah, Cosimo. I'm making coffee,' I say listlessly. I don't want to be rude to Cosimo. He's a good guy.

'Were you expecting me?' he asks.

'No, to tell you the truth. I wasn't expecting anyone.'

'Listen, have a read of this. We're doing a theatre workshop. Do you want to join in?' He holds out a bundle of papers through the bars.

'Why are you asking me?' I don't approach the window or reach out for the papers. That stuff doesn't interest me. I know for this sort of thing there's a particular type of person Cosimo hopes to involve. He wants leaders, people of strong character, people who've got something he can draw out.

'Because you're an artist,' he says simply.

Something runs through my body like a shiver, shakes me up and then passes. As though it never happened, all that remains is the surprise.

'Sure I am. A crime artist,' I say bitterly. 'Please don't make fun of me.'

'Read it.' He waves the pages at me. 'Just read it, okay?'

'What is it?' I don't reach out my hand, but I approach the door.

'It's the script for a play.'

A play? I've never been to the theatre. I've been to the cinema a couple of times, sneaking through the security doors to avoid paying for a ticket. I remember *La boum*, and another film, very dramatic, called *The Balloon Vendor*, which my whole family saw together. We all cried watching it.

'What play?'

'It's Neapolitan. By Eduardo De Filippo—*Napoli milionaria*.'

God, it's that stupid play my parents used to watch every Christmas when they'd show theatre on television. I think of it as old people's theatre, I think of someone sitting on a chair reciting poetry. I think of those teary Christmases when it's cold and you're penniless—you turn on the television and they're screening one of Eduardo's plays.

'Couldn't you find anything more depressing?' I ask sarcastically. 'We're already in prison...'

'It's a beautiful play, and I'd like to give you one of the main parts,' Cosimo says, trying to tempt me.

'Which one?'

'Donna Amalia.'

'What? A woman's part? With all due respect, don Cosimo, you can f—' I swallow the rest of the sentence, turn my back on him and take the coffee maker off the heat because it's about to bubble over.

I hear something dropping to the ground, but I don't turn around. I hear Cosimo walking away and I still don't turn around. When I finally turn to face the door, I see his bundle of papers is there on the floor in front of it. *And you can stay there*, I think. That kind of paper's not even any good for rolling tobacco.

But eventually I do pick it up. I don't like my cell to be messy. I put it on the bedside table. Tomorrow I'll take it back to Cosimo. Me, as Donna Amalia? As if I'm going to get up on stage like a trained monkey. And dressed as a woman as well!

I place the coffee maker on top of it, which means I'll be taking it back to him a bit damaged. That way he'll learn not to throw things into my cell.

The next morning, before I take my drops, curiosity gets the better of me. I've never read anything apart from my legal files, unless you count the odd porno magazine. Let's see what

Eduardo has to say. I take a quick look.

Donna Amalia: 'What do you want from me? I only did what everybody else was doing: I was just defending myself!'

I read that line and it's like I've been hit over the head. I re-read it.

I hear it in my mother's voice.

Then I hear it in mine.

What do you want from me? I only did what everybody else was doing.

You're my son and I died before you—that's what everybody does. You don't have to feel guilty.

I abandoned my mother but only because they were going to kill me. I was just defending myself. What do you want from me?

I turn the pages. And within the story of *Napoli milionaria* I see something new. It's not just the play I used to watch on TV every Christmas with my parents when I was a boy. I find my own life in Naples, people I know. The son Amedeo, who has turned to crime, the daughter Mariarosaria, who whores herself to American soldiers…and Donna Amalia, a woman who loved her little boy before he lost his innocence.

I'm nine years old again and I'm in Standa with my cousin Totò stealing lipstick. And I can see once more the basement of the department store, where the security guard is sticking needles in our hands 'so that we learn not to do it again'. I can see my mother marching towards the store to tear strips off him, to teach *him* not to do it again.

They're just children. Just children…

I've never started anything. I've only ever reacted to the actions of others. Wrong reactions to wrong actions. Perhaps I shouldn't have gone to the store to steal? No, at nine years of age I could go in there and steal. It was my mother who shouldn't have sent me to steal, and the guard who shouldn't have stuck needles in my hands. I shouldn't have sold contraband cigarettes? What about the police that would buy them off me? At the age of nine, how can you tell that something is really wrong if nobody is showing you by example? I was allowed to make mistakes because I didn't know any better. I was just a child. And everybody around me was doing a lot more and a lot worse than I was.

I only did what everybody else was doing.

I absolve myself. The voice of my mother in my head stops insulting me.

What do you want from my mother and me? We were only defending ourselves! And in so doing we hurt ourselves and each other.

After all those weeks, a tear, just one, manages to find its way out of my eye.

6

'We know what we are, but not what we may be.'

Ophelia in *Hamlet*
Act IV, Scene V

'What have you done? Are you trying to kill yourself?'

'I'm fine,' I say, shrugging my shoulders.

'You're mad! You'll destroy your body. Don't you know there's a whole schedule for this sort of thing?' Lucia, the doctor, is astonished, and her eyes show fear.

'I've never been very good at doing what I'm told.'

I've decided to go off the drops. I decided last week while standing in front of the mirror. Was that really me, that dull-eyed rag doll? Swollen, grey, with broken capillaries, my entire face covered in a patina of failure.

'You've become like all the others,' I told myself. At least half the inmates here are on medication; it's their only way of surviving.

And for those in charge, who don't know what to do with us, it's the easiest way to make inmates behave. Except that you can't just find that stuff in a pharmacy, and when you get out, you're still in its clutches. You're enslaved forever.

There are a lot of faces like this one around the prison, I told myself. Too many. You don't need to see yet another one when you look in the mirror. So I reached out and emptied the little medicine bottle down the sink. There's no point trying to give up if it's still full: if you happen to glance at it while you're feeling bad, it only takes a moment to swallow a mouthful of the stuff. If the bottle's empty, you won't have the choice.

'Striano, you can't quit the drops just like that. You have to reduce the dosage in stages.' Lucia's face shows complete incomprehension; to her mind I should have gone insane by now. 'There's a year-long schedule you have to follow to go from 120 drops to zero. Three days at 120, three days at 112, and so on...'

'I don't have that much time at my disposal.'

'What do you mean you don't have that much time?' She's kind, so she doesn't come out and say it, but what she's thinking is that I've got all the time in the world, I'm in prison.

But that was *before*.

'I've got the show.'

'What show?'

'The play. It's on in two weeks. There's no way I could get on stage with my face the way it was.' I slap myself on the cheek, to show her that I'm back in good shape. 'Don't I look handsome now?'

'Striano, have you really cut out the drops just like that? How do you get to sleep?'

'Oh, you know, I tire myself out reading,' I reply truthfully. 'I read and read, and I eventually get tired.'

I can see the look of incredulity on her face, but I really am telling the truth. It's true that I started taking the drops because I couldn't sleep. Night is a prisoner's worst enemy. It's when you're alone, and all your ghosts turn up. The guys in the cell next to mine all take drops because they can still sense Paolo's spirit in there—he hanged himself two weeks ago. They managed to stop him on four previous occasions but the fifth time he did it at 5.40 in the morning, in complete silence. He even put a cushion under the covers so that if they woke up they wouldn't notice the bed was empty. Now nobody can sleep in that cell anymore, not without drops, because they sense that he's there. I can understand that. My mother is still around.

But she no longer scolds me. Now, if she comes I can say to her: *Leave me in peace, Mamma, I'm reading.* I've often fallen asleep with the script on my face. And in the daytime, instead of thinking about my troubles, I think about my lines, about my movements on stage. We have five hours of rehearsal twice a week and I make it a point of honour always to improve something from one rehearsal to the next.

'Striano, you've got to be careful. Go back on the treatment…

You can't be cured instantly,' Lucia tells me.

I nod. 'You can't be cured instantly, it's true. But my treatment's already underway.'

'In what sense? What do you mean?'

'Theatre is my medication, doctor,' and I smile at her the way Donna Amalia would smile.

Don't get me wrong. I had vowed not to get involved in the theatre project. I gave the script back to Cosimo. But before that, I read it four or five times. I couldn't put it down. By the time I returned the script, I knew all the parts. I'd learned a lot of the lines by heart without even realising it.

Cosimo was hanging out his washing on some clothes horses in the yard. A week had passed since he'd left me with that bundle of pages and we hadn't spoken since.

'Cosimo, I don't want to do it...' I told him, holding out the script. 'But what a character, eh, Donna Amalia?'

'Why don't you want to do it?'

'Cosimo, I'm not Donna Amalia, I'm Sasà, look at me—beard, hairy all over...'

'So what? It's the theatre.'

'Sure, some little parish show, with boys playing girls' roles... And everyone else gets to have a laugh—look at that guy, dressed up all slutty.' And to show him what it would be like I recited a couple of Donna Amalia's lines, right there on the spot, with all the gestures and a woman's voice.

He burst out laughing.

'No, that's not theatre! That's pantomime.'

'Exactly.' I became enraged and thrust the script at him. 'And I'm not going to be a caged monkey. I've told you it's not for me. Go find somebody else.'

But Cosimo is not one to give up. The next day he came up to me while I was running in the courtyard. I removed my headphones out of politeness, but I didn't want to listen to him. I could see that he was still holding that script.

'I hope you didn't take offence?'

'What do you think I am, some sensitive actor type who takes offence?'

'I'm sure you'd be good. But you played Donna Amalia too much like a transvestite. It can be done well.'

'Why should I bother?'

'You're like me. You don't like staying cooped up in your cell too long.'

I pricked up my ears. It was true. Being involved in theatre meant getting away from my cell and spending a few hours out in the open. More than that, as I gazed at those sheets of paper in Cosimo's hand, I realised that I'd been missing it. The night before, even though it was only for a few hours, my cell had felt empty without my coffee-stained script. The truth is, it had already begun to keep me company. It was the first cellmate I'd had since arriving in Italy that hadn't made me feel in danger.

I'm holding the crumpled script now, as I enter the rehearsal room. There is a theatre in the prison, but they haven't shown it to us yet; we're rehearsing in a large, empty room until we've learned our lines. From two in the afternoon until seven in the evening, this is our kingdom. Here I can forget that I'm in jail. Here I'm in Naples, in a poor home inhabited by poor people. In some ways, it's a little too close to reality. In other ways it's a completely different reality, and a lot better than life in my cell. This is confusing for me, but it's not a negative feeling. I count the hours until it's time to come back to this room. There are fifteen of us and Cosimo is lead actor and head of the company. Most of us are Neapolitan, as you'd expect. The main female roles, of which there are two, are of course played by men: I'm one of them. We've given the third female role, a small one, to a Calabrian without, shall we say, a great deal of talent.

It took only one rehearsal for me to realise that I do have talent. And that this whole theatre business is something I know better than anything: a challenge.

Here, like elsewhere, I want to show who I am and what I'm capable of. Anyone could see straightaway that I was the most motivated, the one who really gave it his all. Cosimo has been complimenting me a lot on my involvement. He's actually a bit surprised to find that it's often me, not him, who manages to get the others motivated.

Like today with Michele, who is totally distracted and is delivering his lines in random ways.

'What's going on, Miche'? Are you going to do this properly or what?'

'Ah…my visit went badly…' His wife came to see him today,

and there's clearly some kind of problem. Michele places the script on a chair. 'Sorry,' he says, retreating to a seat in the corner.

'All right, let's go on without Michele,' says Cosimo. 'Hey, Sasà. Where are you going?'

Go on without Michele, my arse. In prison there's a very basic principle—if you're doing fine but somebody else is not, then you're not doing fine, either. Prison is where friendships are really glued tight; unlike on the outside, in here people have a true love for others, even if they would ordinarily have nothing to do with each other.

'Hey, what's up?'

'Sasà, leave me be. It's my wife. She's in a bad way.' I can see he's struggling to tell me, partly because it's painful for him, and partly because he's afraid of reopening my old wounds. I'm guessing his wife has the same thing my mother had.

I put an arm around his shoulders. I wouldn't do this anywhere else, but in the rehearsal room these kinds of gestures are easier.

'She's sick, Sasà. And she's all alone,' Michele murmurs. 'It's not just that my wife is dying, but she's going to die alone, without me.'

'I understand,' I say, and I mean it. 'But we made mistakes, Michele. Part of our punishment means not being able to be with our family and friends when they're dying. And you know what? Even people on the outside are unable to be with their family, because they don't have the time. We're not the only bad guys.'

He looks at me in surprise. 'You're so right.'

I'm surprised, too. Where did that come from? Yet it's true, and that's the way it's always been. We only do what everybody else is doing. We make mistakes, we betray others, we leave our loved ones on their own.

'I feel lonely,' Michele adds. 'Even though nothing has happened yet. I feel so lonely.'

'Nobody's alone in prison. At least not like on the outside.' It's true. Here you only have to show that you need a hand and along it comes at once. It's how we show the world, ourselves, the Creator watching us, that we still have some positive energy. We know God exists, that there's some kind of external force. And here you don't experience loneliness unless you're completely rejected by prison society, which means you really are a nasty piece of work. 'You're not alone, Miche'.' I gesture towards the others, who have started rehearsing again, with Cosimo giving me a dirty look every so often because I challenged his authority. 'You've got us. The company.'

'I know, Sasà, thank you...but the thought of rehearsing today, after such a bad visit...'

'What the fuck do I care that you had a bad visit?' Now that he's had some tender treatment he needs to be shaken up a little. I can sense it. 'We need to rehearse,' I add.

My rough voice snaps him out of his lethargy, and he looks at me uncertainly.

'We need to rehearse?'

'You bet we do, no matter what.' And I get up and pull him to his feet as well. 'We're actors, Miche'.'

We *are* actors. Even outside this room we find ourselves talking about the show, about rehearsals, about things that didn't go well and how we can improve. Even when we go out into the yard for exercise hour, we go over our lines.

It gets on everyone else's nerves. They ask us, 'What's going on. Aren't you interested in prison life anymore?'

'It's not that we're not interested. It's just that the theatre project is more important.'

'Fooling around on stage? What's the point of that?'

'Well, for instance, it helps reduce your sentence. It weighs on you less.' The theatre is like a beautiful door, one that prison management can't close.

Or at least that's what we think.

'All recreation activities are suspended.'

'What do you mean, suspended?' I stare at Gaetano. No rehearsals? They're keeping us locked in? What's happened?

'Suspended, Sasà. Isn't that clear enough? No more activities until the warden decides what to do with you all.'

'You lot are never going to work out what to do with us.'

'Sasà, now's not the time to joke around.' I can see that he's nervous. Things must really have turned ugly if he's afraid of being seen acting friendly with me.

'Do you see me laughing?' I reply nastily. The show is on in ten days. What do they mean we can't rehearse? We should be rehearsing twice as much. We're nowhere near ready.

'It's because of that guy who escaped,' Gaetano decides to tell me, though I'd worked that out myself. 'The warden is new, you know how it is…he's only just started here and someone escapes. He doesn't know the prison and until he gets a sense of the lie of the land he's suspending everything.'

'But that's not fair! It's not as though the guy escaped from the theatre!' No, he just strolled right on out, exiting the visiting area. His mother and brother came and they handed over their ID at the entrance, but it's not as though the guards check you again when you come through to collect it on the way out. You say your name, they give it back to you, and they let you out. So out he went in place of his brother, no trouble at all. By the time the guards realised, it was too late, and they couldn't very well lock up his family in his place.

When we first found out, we celebrated—the poor guy was a lifer. But it turns out there was nothing to celebrate. Now what will we do? Apart from having a show to prepare, there's also Federico, a Sicilian kid. He's seriously unbalanced and depressed. Theatre is his only medication. If you cancel rehearsals on him, it's like taking methadone away from a heroin addict. I should go and tell the psychiatrist. Forget about the drops, doctor. This guy is going to kill himself, or somebody else.

I need to talk to don Pasquale.

'Don Pasquale, can I come in?'

'Of course, Sasà, come on in. Can I make you a coffee?'

'I never turn down a coffee.'

Don Pasquale is a man with a heart of gold, and two life

sentences for murder. There's no contradiction in that, it's just the way it is. He's sixty-two years old and he knows that his life is over. He's no longer interested in anything. He doesn't get involved in anything in here, and only confides in two or three people at most. I'm one of them. The other is Leonardo, the guy I stood up for on the football field, who's like a son to him. Ever since that day he has opened his cell door to me, a great honour, and every so often I drop in to say hello, or when I have a problem, like today.

'They've suspended all activities, don Pasquale—the theatre project.'

He nods. 'You need to see things from the warden's point of view. Some fellow escaped when he was based in Padua; now he moves here and it happens again.' I don't know how, but don Pasquale always knows everything. 'He's walking on eggshells.'

'But we didn't do anything.'

'If you didn't do anything you wouldn't be in here.'

'Don Pasquale, don't take it out on me. I'm worried about the show.'

'Why?' he asks point-blank, fixing those dark eyes on me, as deep as a bottomless well.

'Why?'

'Why are you so interested in this?'

I hesitate. It's a good question. But there's a complex answer.

'Because it's bringing out the people with talent, don Pasquale. And I've got talent,' I say, with conviction. 'On stage, you're good not because of what you did on the outside, but because of what you're doing right there and then. It's not like football with the Sicilians.'

'That lot win even when they lose,' he says with a smile, and a little bit of proud parochialism.

The Sicilians are crazy when it comes to football. Even if you tear them to pieces in the match, they still don't feel beaten. 'Do you know who we are?' they say. 'You might have won the match, but we've got the Mafia.' What do you say to that?

'Uh-huh. But it's different in rehearsals. What matters is what you can do.' Then I add, out of love for the truth, 'Except for the Poet, who thinks he's better than everyone because he's been inside the longest.' The Poet is a man named Giulio. He's insufferable—I even got into a fight with him once.

'Could it be that this Donna Amalia has found a little place in your heart?' don Pasquale says, to provoke me.

'I like Donna Amalia because she's good,' I admit. 'And because she explains things. I've never given or received explanations in my life. Plus...' I stop. I've already bored him to shits with the story of my mother. But he presses me to go on.

'Plus?'

'Plus, I took my mother as my model,' I mumble. 'I rehearse in my cell thinking about how she used to say things, how she moved, how she stirred her coffee, how she handled the dish-cloth...all those wonderful things about her. Don Pasquale, taking away our rehearsals is like taking away visiting time. It's cruel. They can't do this.'

He slowly pours the coffee, concentrating, as though it's a ritual. He looks into the darkness of the cup and who knows what he sees there. Perhaps he sees a time when something mattered to him the way this play matters to us now.

'Shut yourselves up in your cells,' he says in the end.

I open my eyes wide. He hasn't understood the problem.

'Well actually, we're already shut up in our cells,' I say, trying to maintain a respectful tone. I'd never be rude to don Pasquale. He can turn me to stone with a single glance. 'We need to come out to be able to rehearse.'

'I understand the problem,' he retorts harshly. 'And the solution is that you all stay in your cells and you tell the warden. You tell him: "We understand that you're in difficulty, and that you have to work out which doors to open and which to close. And until you work that out we'll stay in our cells, so as not to cause you further headaches."'

'And do you think then he'll open things up again?'

'I think he'll see that you're not trying to screw him over, that he can trust you. And then he'll open things up.'

And so it goes. We put together a nice little delegation—as usual, a Sicilian, a Neapolitan, a Calabrian, an Apulian, a Roman and a foreigner—and we go to see the warden and explain to him that we're staying in our cells to help him, that we won't be coming out for visits or anything. Two days later, recreational activities start up again.

And there's a surprise awaiting us in the rehearsal room.

o

'This director here wants to watch us rehearse.' Cosimo introduces the new arrival, a distinguished man with very short white hair, a straight nose and a little bit of stubble.

'If you'd like a hand, that's what I'm here for,' is all the man says. His name is Fabio Cavalli and he's a theatre director, he explains.

Some of us are wary. It's our first time rehearsing in front of a stranger. What does this guy want? How exactly does he want to help us?

'All right, let's get going. We don't have a lot of time,' I say eventually, cutting to the chase like I always do.

At the end of the rehearsal Cavalli gathers us round and says, 'You're really crap.'

There are murmurs of protest—we've given it our all. What the fuck does this guy want?

'We can work on you,' the director says, pointing at me. 'But as for the rest of you, look, you're irredeemable. Just as well they've locked you away.'

I'm expecting an explosion, but he's spoken so frankly that we kind of have to laugh. We stare at each other. We're all wearing wigs because we're embarrassed to get on stage looking like ourselves. We've been told there will be TV cameras and we're afraid that people at home will see us, and that someone who didn't know we were in prison will end up finding out. We're afraid of jogging the memory of someone testifying to the public prosecutor, and we're afraid of embarrassing ourselves. Well, we ought to be embarrassed done up in these wigs, those of us dressed as women with our faces painted, too.

Cavalli goes on, before he can lose too much ground. 'Guys, I'd take sincerity as a starting point. I'd begin with the courage that Sasà is showing in not feeling silly.'

'Silly? *Moi?* Is there something wrong with your eyes?' I protest in an injured tone, touching my hair in an affected way. And they all burst out laughing.

I'm a born actor, no two ways about it.

'I only want to give you some advice,' Cavalli continues, once the laughter and catcalls have died down. 'If you're willing to take it. Get rid of this gear that makes you look like the Taliban...' He points at the wigs and scarves we're hiding under. 'You're unrecognisable like that.'

'But we *want* to be unrecognisable!' the Poet objects. 'So they don't see us at home...'

'You don't need to be embarrassed or afraid,' Cavalli insists. 'Be serious about this. Behave like actors.'

We're not convinced, so we find a compromise. We'll act in our disguises, because they make us feel safer, but after the last line, each of us will slowly take off his wig. The man beneath will appear.

I like this idea.

Donna Amalia will appear on stage, but so will Sasà.

When I finally step onto the stage I realise at once that perhaps for the first time in my life, I'm right where I belong. On performance night, after just a few rehearsals in the theatre, I feel like

I've been acting in the theatre forever.

The audience claps every time I come on stage, and after each of my lines. It's holding things up, and we have to keep stopping until the applause dies down. I pause after my line, with a funny expression on my face. I can hear them going crazy. They're applauding me. They're saying 'bravo' to me, the man everyone used to be afraid of. I feel the enthusiasm, the waves of love arriving along with the applause. It's better than any drug.

When I take my wig off at the end, slowly, as planned, and stand there with my face bared to them all, my eyes are full of tears. I see Monica, sitting in the third row, holding the red rose that I'd asked one of the volunteers to bring for her. She's smiling at me like never before.

At the end of the performance, officials and professionals come backstage. I think some are important figures in the arts, but I don't know who any of them are. There's one name I do know, though—Luca De Filippo, the son of Eduardo. The master's son is here in person. He says, 'I'm staging *Napoli milionaria* outside, at the Teatro Argentina. I hope my actress will forgive me if I say that the way you do Donna Amalia…It only took you three minutes to make me forget that there was a man under that costume.'

'Now I know why I can never find good actors for my films,' says another man, a director. 'They're all in jail!'

An old lady who had been sitting in the front row takes my hand and kisses it. She kisses my hand!

'Signora, what are you doing?'

'Bravo,' is all she says. 'Bravo.'

It's all over too fast. After only five minutes the guards separate us from the audience and make us return to our cells. Why are you doing this to us? Haven't we earned the accolades? It casts a shadow over the best night of my life.

Still, back in my cell I cry tears of joy. I cry all night.

INTERMEZZO

When I was little I experienced the streets as a stage. I headed into the street in the morning and I had to be an actor in all sorts of stories, but I hadn't written or chosen the script. Treading the boards of the real stage, in the theatre, is different. It's a thousand sensations rolled into one.

On stage, someone like me can think: From up here I really have a chance to make it in the world. *On stage I stand before you, the audience, and say: 'This is all I am and you alone are my judges, you must judge me.' On stage I have the sense that I can attain forgiveness.*

And I feel guappo, *I mean truly* guappo: *powerful, important. I feel taller. I have a perspective from which I look out over the world like a giant and I can say to anyone: 'Hey, what do you want?' And I mean, say it well, say it without fear.*

Here in prison they don't know what to do with me. In prison you can only become one thing: a crime connoisseur. An encyclopaedia. Because all the discussions that take place, all the anecdotes people tell, are crime stories. They can be frightening or boring, instructional or stupid, but that's all you talk about. You take your own dumb story into a prison and in return you get the other dumb stories. But all you're doing is exchanging poison.

We need different stories. Bigger than the ones we grew up with, capable of helping us understand how we ended up in here.

I went straight from reality to the stage. I've never seen theatre or read books, and I've never had any stories to consume; instead, reality consumed me. Perhaps that's why, for me, the veil between life and performance is thinner. On stage I don't give you an actor's performance. I give you, directly, everything I am.

You ask: 'Had you really never acted before?'

And I reply: 'Guys, I've been acting all my life.'

But this time it's different. You got me involved, got me reading, put a script in my hand? Well, now I'm going to show you who I am.

I don't want to come down from this stage.

PART THREE
THE TEMPEST

'I hold the world but as the world, Gratiano,
A stage, where every man must play a part.'

Antonio in *The Merchant of Venice*
Act I, Scene I

7

'My library
Was dukedom large enough.'

Prospero in *The Tempest*
Act I, Scene II

'So who is this, anyway?'

The room is a cacophony of voices. Cavalli has really done it this time. For our next show, instead of a play by Eduardo, he's brought along a script by some Shapesgear, or Spakesheer, or some other unpronounceable name. Who is this fellow and what's he got to tell us?

'He's one of the greatest playwrights of all time, dammit!' exclaims the director, as if we'd just insulted his mother. 'You can't be such donkeys that you've never heard of Shakespeare!'

'Yeah, nice name. Shakes-Beer!' The jibes start flying thick and fast as we compete to see who can best mangle this intruder's surname. Shakes-Beer does make me laugh. Then I think, poor guy, he's a foreigner. He can't help it if he's got stupid name. So I change my line of attack.

'But listen, Fabio. What kind of story is this? A bunch of Spaniards get shipwrecked on an island, there's a sorcerer, a spirit of the air…I mean come on. What does this have to do with us?' My tone is reasonable, I don't want to come right out and tell him he has screwed up, but this play is completely wrong. While he was telling us the story and reading the first few lines, the others couldn't stop yawning.

Fabio stares at me as if to say, 'I didn't expect this from you.' But instead he says: 'Do you want to know why you're *exactly* the people to be putting on this play? What it's got to do with you?'

'Well, yeah,' I reply, without averting my gaze, but a little unnerved by the intensity of his.

'For one reason, and one alone.' His tone quietens all those voices making fun of Shakespeare, so that the next few words fall upon an eerie silence. 'It's about vendetta, forgiveness and freedom.'

I am silent, too. I never had much faith in words until I began this theatre thing. Now I'm starting to understand their value. And these are three heavyweight words. One of them we know well. One we've never encountered. And the third is not a part of our lives at all.

I remain uncertain. I feel like those words struck me physically. In any case, nobody is convinced. Ours is a theatre company started up by two Neapolitans, composed mostly of Neapolitans: hands off Eduardo.

'Fabio, we're loyal to Eduardo!' This time it's Cosimo speaking, maybe in part so that I'm not the only one taking the initiative. He doesn't like it when I speak on behalf of the group or when the others come to me; he wants to be the only leader. I let him speak. The theatre company was his idea, after all. I don't care about appearing to be in charge. I just want the guys to deliver their lines properly and for us to perform like professionals.

However, I agree with Cosimo. Eduardo De Filippo brought us success and we will not betray him. He wrote dozens of beautiful plays, enough to keep us busy for the length of our sentences, even the lifers.

'We won't disrespect him in this way. We have our code of honour,' Cosimo adds decisively. There are shouts and whistles of agreement and approval.

Cavalli looks at us. We're all against him.

'You're talking like gangsters,' he says contemptuously.

'Well actually, Fabio,' sneers Francesco, a Sicilian, 'we *are* gangsters.'

'What you are is a bunch of dickheads,' says the director as he gets to his feet. 'Do whatever you like.'

He slams the door behind him, leaving the script there on the table.

We start celebrating like we've held off the worst kind of enemy—the English invader—and discussing which will be the next Eduardo play we put on.

But as we leave, I walk past the table and take the script with me. Nobody needs it, and I don't mind the idea of having something else to read in my cell. *The Tempest*. Ridiculous story. Nice title, though.

Over the next few days I don't open the play because I have other things to read. I'm loyal to Eduardo like everyone else, but Cavalli's words really struck me, and made me think that there's still so much I don't know. We're gangsters and we're ignorant—how is it possible I've never even heard the name of this unpronounceable author, this Shakespeare guy? And who knows how many other writers are out there? Maybe even some talented playwrights.

What if there were other plays as good as Eduardo's? That would be hard. But what if we could find one everybody would agree on? I might even be the one to find it.

I enter the prison library, uneasy—I still feel weighed down by the thought that I'm betraying Eduardo.

'Hi, Bennett.'

The librarian nods. He's a Nigerian man, very tall and hand-some, and highly educated.

'Sasà, I've never seen you here before. What are you after?'

'Oh, it's just that now we've done *Napoli milionaria*, we have to choose something for our next performance,' I explain. 'I wanted to look at some books, see what's out there.'

As I say it I realise it's a crazy undertaking. There really are heaps of books in here. And who knows how many more there are on the outside. I feel dizzy: where do I even start?

'Have you got something particular in mind?' he asks kindly.

'No, I'll just take a look around,' I say, in the same way you reply to the sales assistant in a clothes shop. I don't want him to see that I have no idea where to even put my hands. I might be ignorant, but I have my dignity.

I park myself in front of a bookshelf and run my eyes along the titles until I finally find one I recognise. Sure, I could take this one. I've often heard of it but I've never read it. I don't think it's right for the theatre, but at least this way I can save face. It's a start, as they say. And while I'm here I grab another thick book, one with a soft cover: *The Godfather*. It says it's a novel, so who knows if it will tell things like they really are.

I go back to the table with my loot and hand it over to Bennett, whose eyes open wide.

'No, Sasà!' He looks at me and shakes his head violently. 'Forget about this one, it's not for you!'

His tone is really worried. What an overreaction.

'What, *The Godfather*? You think it's going to give me bad ideas?' I'm smiling, to let him know that, sure, books are important, but you don't need to make a big drama about it.

'No, not *The Godfather*, that's not a problem.' With his chin he indicates the other book, like he doesn't even want to touch it. '*This* the one you shouldn't take. It's a bad book.'

'*The Divine Comedy*?'

'That's right. Forget about Dante.'

'But he's really famous. People always talk about him…'

I'm confused. How come it's yes to *The Godfather* but no to *The Divine Comedy*? What sort of a librarian is he? Is he on something? Impossible. Bennett doesn't even smoke.

'Yes, he's the most famous writer there is, but he's also the biggest bastard of them all,' he retorts. 'This guy is not for us, Sasà. He destroys us, burns us, cuts us into little pieces, makes us suffer. This guy sends us to hell.'

He seems really convinced. But I've always been the kind of person who becomes more determined to do something the more you tell me not to do it. It's not arrogance, but nobody should think they can give me their opinion and that's that. I'll hear you out, but I'll think for myself and respond, and maybe I'll even be able to change your mind. So I say to Bennett, 'Well, I'll read it and let you know.'

In resignation, he records the loan and says goodbye.

I set off with Dante under my arm and I can feel Bennett's eyes on my back, just like my mother's when she would watch me head out in bad company, knowing that I was going to get mixed up in some kind of trouble.

Over the next two weeks I read Dante and I begin to understand what Bennett meant when he said he was the biggest bastard of them all. There's something that doesn't add up with this Dante sending everybody to hell. He takes all life's problems out of the mix and puts everything in order, but there's no compassion. As I read I imagine him as a priest in a long cassock, stern and grim, throwing each person into their circle of hell. He's not speaking to me, he's judging me. Maybe somebody chaste and pure can feel protected by Dante; they might like his obsession with creating order. I just feel the desire to rebel.

When I get to the canto about Paolo and Francesca, who are blown back and forth on the wind unable to touch each other, just because they fell in love, a lump forms in my throat. I think about Monica, and all of us in here separated from the ones we love. One on either side of a wall, we breathlessly squeeze each other's hands. Every inmate is Paolo with his Francesca, and love is something we can only remember with regret, in the windswept silence of our own hell.

I feel the pain rising, and with it a rage so great that I wish I had Dante right here in front of me so I could tell him a thing or two about life.

No, my dear Dante, I'm not going into one of your circles of hell. I've done all sorts of things in my life, so I'd like to see where you'd decide to put me. You'd stick me in one circle, and then you'd realise that I fit better in another, and then in another one again…And once I'd done the rounds of all your circles, you know where I belong, Dante? Outside.

'Don Pasquale, do you think it's a problem that I used to talk to my dead mother of an evening, but now I talk to Dante?' I give my coffee a stir.

'Dante who?' I can see him trying to bring to mind an inmate by the name of Dante.

'Dante Alighieri.'

'What, the poet?' he asks, wide-eyed.

'Er…' I stare at my coffee for a moment because I'm embarrassed. 'I've started reading *The Divine Comedy* and there's something that just doesn't sit right with me.'

'Something that doesn't sit right with you? Sasà, look at me,' he says in a worried tone. 'Could it be that you're feeling guilty?'

'Guilty? Me? What for?'

'Maybe for placing bets on the dead.'

I'm startled. The man never leaves his cell, yet don Pasquale always knows everything.

'You know you shouldn't, Sasà,' he adds sternly.

'But don Pasquale, it's just a social thing…' I mumble, but I do feel guilty. At the moment in Naples there's an ugly turf war going on between the Camorra clans, and each day we place bets on who will be the next person to get taken out. When we watch the evening news, the winner is whoever guessed right, and last night I won two ice-creams.

'It's disrespectful. Towards the dead and towards those who suffer,' don Pasquale says reproachfully. 'Maybe that's why you're feeling guilty. Your problem's not with Dante, but with your own conscience.'

'Don Pasquale, you're right that I shouldn't make those bets, and I won't do it anymore,' I reply. 'But you're wrong about Dante, and I say that with respect. My problem with Dante is that he gets God all mangled.'

'Sasà, what are you saying?' he thunders. He can't abide blasphemy. But I'm convinced of what I'm talking about and I have to make him understand.

'No, really. It's like Dante's interrogating me as I read. He asks me all my sins and makes me name them like I'm in confession. But he doesn't offer any divine mercy, don Pasquale. He doesn't follow the laws of God.' I'm venting, getting more and more heated. 'He makes me confess and then he tells me I have to suffer, burn, perish. And that's not right.'

My cell neighbour looks at me long and hard, then shakes his head.

'Sasà, maybe you need to start taking all this reading a bit less personally,' he says. 'Let me have a think about another poet to recommend to you. In the meantime, do you have anything else to read in your cell, so you can put Dante to one side for a bit?'

'I did have *The Godfather* but I've finished it. Good story, but nothing we don't already know, don Pasquale.' I hesitate for a moment. 'I've got a play by this English guy...'

'And what's the name of this English guy?'

'His name is Shakespeare.' I've been seeing it on the table for so long I've even learned how to spell it, and I try to reproduce Cavalli's pronunciation. 'William Shakespeare. Cavalli, the theatre director, reckons this *Tempest* play of his is about us.'

Don Pasquale nods. 'Cavalli is right, Sasà. *The Tempest* is all about us.'

Meanwhile, though, at our theatre meetings, Shakespeare's name hasn't come up again. Cavalli has given up the fight; he knows we want to do more De Filippo. And besides, if we don't, what will we say to his wife, Donna Isabella? She became so fond of us after *Napoli milionaria* that she gave us some of the furniture from the original performance. When Luca De Filippo put the play on at the Teatro Argentina, he had to get a whole new set because we had the original! Donna Isabella gave us the bed and also the dressing table where Eduardo used to get ready. She even gave me the scarf I wore over my head as Donna Amalia, and I keep it like a treasure. We're men of principle, we have rules, we have values and we won't betray Eduardo De Filippo. We're thinking about our next play— together we've read *I Won't Pay You* and *Mayor of Sanità Alley*; it's hard to decide on one, but we're full of ideas.

Then one day Cavalli gathers us all in the theatre, not the rehearsal room. There before us is Luca De Filippo. We haven't seen him since the night we performed *Napoli milionaria*.

'First of all I want to reiterate how much I admire your work,' he begins. 'I'll be honest with you. I came to see *Napoli milionaria* as a gesture of solidarity, because you'd chosen one of my father's plays. And I left greatly taken aback. You're actors. Real actors.'

This is true for some more than others, but hearing it from the son of the great Eduardo De Filippo opens our hearts. But is it possible he's come here several weeks later just to compliment us on our performance? And that's when he knocks us out with what he has to say.

'But now you have a problem,' he goes on. 'A serious problem.' Huh?

'What problem do we have, if you don't mind us asking?' I chime in. 'We want to do another De Filippo play—don't you like the idea?'

'Of course I like the idea…You fill me with pride,' he says, smiling. 'And my father will be the happiest man in the world if he's looking down at us from the stars above. But I want to tell you a story. When I was fifteen, sixteen years old, I spent all my time around my father because I'd already decided I wanted to work in theatre, too. I wanted to dedicate my life to it. And that is how, through my father, I got to know Shakespeare.'

'What, the English guy?' is the general mumble around the room. 'So Eduardo De Filippo knew him too? But hasn't he been dead a bunch of centuries?'

'That's the one,' Luca nods. 'My father was a great fan of Shakespeare. As a son, I feel so honoured to see the respect and affection you have for my father. But as an artist, and because I want to see you grow, I have to tell you that to become the great Eduardo De Filippo, there was a point in my father's career when he turned to the works of Shakespeare.'

'With all due respect,' a voice booms from behind me, and I recognise it immediately as the Poet's, 'you're not just trying to flatter us, are you? Because you're so keen to make us like this Shapesgear?'

'No, that's not it, and I can prove it,' De Filippo says resolutely.

'Prove it?'

'Yes.' And he pulls another of those bundles of pages from his bag, with the smile of a poker player putting down straight aces. 'You see, the only play by another person that my father ever worked on was *The Tempest*.'

'Did he translate it from English into Italian?' I ask. After talking to don Pasquale I had started reading the script in secret, in my cell, but I didn't realise De Filippo translated the play, too...

'He translated it into seventeenth-century Neapolitan dialect.' Luca De Filippo nods. 'Very few people know this, and nobody has ever staged it. My father died before he was able to do so himself.'

'And why haven't you, his son, ever done it?' Fabio Cavalli asks. He and Luca have clearly prepared this question beforehand.

'Eduardo's wife, Isabella, preferred that I didn't,' Luca says a little sadly. 'But I've asked her and she says she would give you permission. She would give you the rights to stage Shakespeare's *The Tempest* in Eduardo De Filippo's Neapolitan translation.' And he thumps the bundle of pages, grabbing everybody's attention. It is as though the spirit of Eduardo De Filippo himself was emanating from those pages. 'Shakespeare died shortly after writing this play,' Luca adds in a pensive voice. 'And my father, likewise, was never able to see it performed. You can do it, for him. Your performance would be a world premiere.'

A world premiere in a prison. You don't need to be as cultured as don Pasquale to realise that would be amazing. We all fall silent. Not even Cavalli speaks, leaving us to take in the dramatic effect.

'Well, if we're sure it would be fine with him…' Cosimo ventures. 'With De Filippo, I mean…that we wouldn't be showing him any disrespect…'

Luca De Filippo bursts out laughing, releasing some of the tension that had built up with his revelation about *The Tempest*.

'You guys are great,' he says. 'And, on behalf of my father, I thank you. Trust me, you're embracing Shakespeare. My father will be happy.'

Now that we've resolved the problem of the code of honour, I must say I'm happy, too. When I started reading *The Tempest* I realised something. We love Eduardo, but he's inadvertently making our situation worse. He writes about our world, and he makes family tragedies familiar in a way that is immediately comprehensible to us. Whereas Shakespeare…Reading him was like diving into a body of water when I couldn't even see the bottom. It was like diving into something bigger than I've ever encountered before.

We allowed Eduardo into our group, and he became our leader. But in doing that we were locking ourselves up again. Forming another gang. It was just another way never to come out. This is what Cavalli meant when he tried to present Shakespeare to us: 'Theatre allows you to face up to your feelings.' Feelings, not situations.

'All right, then,' I say, to whittle away any remaining resistance. 'Let's put on Eduardo's *Tempest*, not Shakespeare's.'

This gets everyone in agreement. And 'Shakes-Beer' is officially accepted.

However, I now have a problem. And I don't want to leave here without resolving it. 'Fabio, that script you left with me the other day, I read it a bit,' I begin. Cosimo gives me a dirty look, as if I'd somehow exploited an unfair advantage. 'I know you were happy with the way I played Donna Amalia but...you're not going to want me to play Miranda in this new show, are you? Because it's one thing to be a good actor, but I really don't think I'd be at my best playing a young virgin in love.'

They all burst out laughing and Fabio reassures me. 'I might be able to get a woman to sign up for the role of Miranda,' he says.

'A real woman? In here?' An uproar ensues and it's hard to tell if people are more attracted or frightened by the idea.

'You guys are good, but that role is too important,' says Fabio. 'No one among you is so amazing an actor as to be able to carry it off. Sasà, you've read the play. Which role would you like?' I know he's asking me in order to get people fully accustomed to the idea that we're putting on *The Tempest*. Once we start assigning roles, it's a done deal. That's fine with me, as I already know which role I want.

I begin, 'Well, actually, I—' but Cosimo cuts me off.

'Sasà would be perfect as one of the servants,' he says resolutely.

'What, Stephano and Trinculo?' Cavalli is astonished. 'But they're minor roles! You want to give such a small part to the best actor in the company?'

'Fine then, let him play Prospero!' replies Cosimo, offended.

'No way!' I intervene, trying to placate everybody. I already know all too well that Cosimo will want to play Prospero, the sorcerer, the great leader. I can understand it, and frankly I couldn't care less because that's not what I'm interested in. 'Ariel's the one I like.'

'You want to play Ariel? Why's that?' Cavalli is intrigued.

'He seems strong. I like the way he clutches at freedom. He becomes so servile because he has one goal: his freedom, which is what each of us in here values most highly.' It is something I've thought about a lot.

'It's decided, then,' says Cavalli, ignoring the fact that Cosimo is white with rage. 'You'll be Ariel.' Those words almost sound like magic. Something tells me that our little theatre company has changed in a flash: we've upped the ante. And I imagine I can feel in my ear, like a passing breeze, the crystalline laugh of the spirit of the air. Or could it even be Shakespeare I hear?

8

'Things base and vile, holding no quantity,
Love can transpose to form and dignity'

Elena in *A Midsummer Night's Dream*,
Act I, Scene I

'The thing about you is, you've got no shame. You're shameless.
You're brazen.'

I can't blame Bennett. After visiting the library so often for
weeks, I managed to drag him into the theatre group. He gave
me a great gift, and continues to do so every day: he's helping
me discover the magic of books, lending me the ones he thinks
I might like and keeping me away from others. In exchange,
I decided to give him a taste of magic, too. The magic of the
stage. But Cosimo has given him the role of Stephano, and he's
puzzled.

'Read through all the lines and then we can talk about it,' I suggest, and then I go and rehearse my scene with Prospero, where I first ask him for my freedom. I wonder how long it will be till I stop feeling a lump in my throat every time I say that word. A word that doesn't belong to me.

What Bennett says is true: I've got no shame when I perform. Why not? It's something I realised when I got up on stage in front of an audience, when the lights went up and I saw their eyes. When I heard their applause. For the first time in my life I was being recognised for something good. For something I could be proud of, instead of something negative, something wrong, something criminal. It was like a revolution. I finally understood how much shame I'd felt before, deep down. It was like breaking a chain.

Now that I'm Ariel, I'm no longer ashamed of myself.

It's different for the others. It's not so easy for them to get into character. Some can't manage it at all. Especially the Calabrians and the Apulians. They're really tense, and barely open their mouths. It's almost impossible for them to get inside a character's head. They have constant problems delivering their lines.

'But why do I have to insult him? I don't use that kind of language!'

'It's not you saying it. It's the character!'

The short circuit between Shakespeare and the Calabrian code of conduct risks derailing the entire show. And let's not even talk about the Sicilians.

'"You are men of sin!" If you want to escape the "lingering

perdition", the "wraths" about to be unleashed on you, you have repent and live honestly!' I declaim passionately, addressing the actors playing Alonso, Antonio and Sebastian. I'm standing on top of one of the bunk beds that we're using as a set and they're looking up at me in astonishment. They've been convicted of murder, drug trafficking and Mafia association.

They throw their scripts on the ground.

'Sasà, what are you saying? We're supposed to *repent*?' Lello, who is playing Antonio, has got his hackles up.

'Poor Sasà, first they make you play a chick, and now an *infame*...' Daniele, who's playing Alonso, is sympathetic. 'But we're not playing *infami*, we're not naming names!'

'Nobody has to name names,' I explain patiently.

'Look, if you're going to repent you have to name names, that's the way it works,' Lello explains equally patiently.

Of course! For them, *pentito*—someone who repents—is a dirty word. For them a *pentito* is someone who collaborates with police, naming former associates in exchange for a lighter sentence.

'I meant "repent" in the sense of repenting for what you've done, I didn't mean collaborating with the police...You can't tell me you haven't repented, that you're not still repenting for what happened in the past? Don't you feel anything holding this in your hand?' I wave their scripts around passionately.

'Oh, repent in *that* sense...' Lello mumbles. They take back their scripts but I can see they're still not really convinced.

Cosimo is the one who should be taking care of this, after

he's head of the company, but the point is they come to me with these sorts of problems. They rely on me because I'm the most easygoing, the most positive, and also the only one who has already memorised his lines, and not just my own but sometimes theirs as well. They come to me when they don't know how to deliver a line, when they need help with the complexities of the plot, or how to play their role. Or when they simply don't want to play their role.

'I don't want to play a drunk,' Bennett insists, and this time Renatino, who is supposed to be playing Trinculo, joins in. 'Neither do I,' he adds.

They look at me belligerently and hand me their scripts, which I take without a word. I feel like saying 'Okay, leave then. If you don't get it, go back to your cells.' I can't solve all the company's problems, and Cosimo gets resentful when he sees the others confiding in me.

But what would Ariel do? Ariel wouldn't leave them on the beach alone. Ariel goes and speaks to these two men: after all, he's the one who unleashed the tempest.

I take them aside.

'Guys, do you understand who Stephano and Trinculo are?'

'They're a couple of drunks,' says Bennett, a teetotaller, in a tone of deep disapproval. 'Two stupid idiots on a crazy bender.'

'Huh,' I nod, choosing not to contradict them. 'But have you thought about the kind of life they'd been leading? On that ship, they were stuck down in the hold, locked up. Above deck were these noblemen, these dukes, who would only call on them so they could order them about. Then when the tempest is unleashed, and the ship is wrecked, in these guys' heads, right, it's a storm for everybody else, but for them it's a party. On the ship they were servants but when they make it onto the island, that means freedom!'

'But...so...they're like us?' asks Renatino, his face lighting up.

'These two are the only ones who are like us,' I say with conviction. 'All the rest of them are guards.'

'But Stephano and Trinculo hatch a plot with Caliban,' Bennett protests.

'Caliban manipulates them, taking advantage of their euphoria,' I point out. 'He tells Trinculo that he should become leader of the island...He's playing on their simplicity, but also on the fact that they're so excited to finally be free. You see, these two are the only guys on the island without a care and with nothing to hide. No fear, no guilt, no remorse, no conspiracies. They're the only ones who are truly free.'

I know for sure that I've convinced them, I can see it in their eyes. Renatino's are shining bright.

'The only free characters in the whole show,' I repeat decisively. 'The only ones who, right from the start, can express their relief, their joy. Take that joy, take it.' I hand them their scripts. 'Take it all.'

I know that, as Ariel, I'll almost always be on their side. I know already that it will be a pleasure to see these two prisoners take hold of the freedom that Shakespeare, with these two characters, threw into his play.

'Hey, this Antonio guy, what kind of a look does he have on his face?' I've only just finished with those two when Lello pipes up again. 'Am I supposed to let on that I want to kill my brother, or not?'

I'm starting to tire of this. It's not like I was born in the theatre, and anyway, I've got enough on my hands with my own character. Sure, I seem to know intuitively what to do. But knowing what everybody else should be doing too is a whole other thing.

'Don't worry about your character,' I tell Lello. 'Think about Prospero instead.'

'Prospero? But I want to kill him.'

'Uh-huh. And just think, he forgives you twice over. Work with this, the fact that Prospero forgives you twice. Once, when you set him and his daughter adrift on a boat, not knowing if he'd survive—because you had no guarantee he was going to find an island where he could land and start his life over. And the second time, when you meet up again on the island and try with Alonso to kill him a second time.

'It's true…' Lello murmurs, and I can see that he's starting to understand. 'So I can be as nasty as I like?'

'Exactly! You can be completely unscrupulous. He's going to forgive you all the same!' I know, it's a non-actor's explanation, but we're talking about a prison inmate here. The only advice I can give him is: show us the worst side of yourself, the nastiest. Do what off stage can't be done, what you wish you'd never done. That is the magic of theatre. 'Don't worry about what you're supposed to do. No matter what you do, he'll forgive you, so who gives a fuck?'

'I can make Antonio real vicious?' Lello's face lights up.

'As vicious as you like. You can even cut Prospero up into little pieces, but he has to forgive you. It's written here—' I thump the script with the back of my hand '—that he forgives you. How good is that?'

'I'll twist his head off!' He goes off, happy as can be, to practise his part while to my right I hear Valentina's voice ring out, 'Why can't you hug me, for heaven's sake?'

I turn around. Valentina is one of the two women, volunteers who Cavalli, as promised, managed to convince to join our theatre company. Ever since our performance of *Napoli milionaria*, newspapers and TV channels have taken a huge interest in us, and as soon as they discovered that for the next show the director is going to stick two women in with a bunch of maximum-security inmates, they've been falling over themselves to interview Valentina, the younger one, who is our Miranda. How does she handle these coarse men, these criminals, they ask her. Is it very hard to make them keep their hands to themselves?

She replies with another question: 'Coarse, that lot? Why don't the rest of you men go inside for a bit and take a few lessons in manners and how to treat women?' I'm not sure what she says is true, that we're so incredibly polite. But I do know that we respect women, and wouldn't so much as touch her with a single finger without permission.

That includes Federico, who is our Ferdinand in the play. As a Sicilian, he wouldn't dream of breaching the code of honour. The thing is, though—just a minor detail—in *The Tempest* he's meant to be her beloved.

'You have to touch me. Embrace me, for heaven's sake!' Valentina begs him, so frustrated she's almost in tears.

We've all been really envious of him—when you're on the inside, having a woman to embrace is a kind of mirage—but now we envy him a little less. He's faced with a tricky problem. I'm not going to step in this time because, frankly, I wouldn't know how to advise him.

'Federico, you have to be more affectionate,' says Cavalli, who until now has been off to one side speaking to Cosimo in hushed tones about Prospero.

Federico looks at him with his big blue eyes. He's a good-looking guy, a little over thirty.

'More affectionate,' he repeats disconsolately.

'Well yes, Ferdinand is in love with Miranda!' Valentina is gentle in her insistence. She places a hand on his shoulder and he jumps. 'You have to make me feel the love.'

'Valentina, what do I know about love?' he replies softly, as though ashamed, but we all hear it because we've fallen completely silent. 'I've been in here since I was eighteen years old. I'm all alone…'

We're pitiful, I realise, suddenly seeing for the first time what a sorry bunch we are. We evoke tenderness, and pity. Our specialties are battles, murder, hatred and betrayal—and we're perfectly at home with them. The problem comes when we have to show love.

I start to wonder if we mightn't have taken on a bit more than we can handle with Shakespeare. It's something too different from all that we've ever known and all that we've ever been. Something that will change us. That's already changing us.

'Hey Ariel, can you come over here a minute?'

'All hail, great master! I come to answer thy best pleasure. What is it?'

I've now well and truly become Ariel for everybody in our section of the prison. I recently took up a job so I'm not locked up all day. Every morning at seven, and every evening at eight, I leave my cell early to do the cleaning. It gives me a chance to shower twice a day, so I'm always clean, even in the height of summer. There is no bathroom in your room when you're in prison, and you only get free access to the bathrooms if you're allowed out of your cell. I wake up and I wash these nice, long stretches of tiles, and then I go for a half-hour run, have a shower, and go to school. Since I started reading, I've decided to go back to study as well, and in a year I should be able to graduate from middle school. Then, with all the time I've got left in here, I should be able to get a technical diploma. That is, as long as they don't go too heavy on the maths, which really isn't my forte.

Anyway, since I'm out and about I visit all the cells to see if anyone needs anything: maybe a packet of pasta or coffee, or some cigarettes. If someone new has arrived overnight, I check whether he needs anything to tide him over until the next round of shopping. The previous worker didn't offer this service, but I consider it my duty. Being the only one allowed out and not checking if the others need anything just isn't my style. It's not Ariel's style.

'Everything all right, Ariel?' Gaetano asks.

'You bet!' I give him a slap on the back. Another thing I would never have dreamed of doing before. But since we've been doing theatre, everything has changed, even relations with the guards. Gaetano, who got himself assigned to supervise rehearsals and practically knows the whole play off by heart, looks at us differently now, but so do the other guards.

'We know that you never get mixed up in anything dodgy,' they told me when they realised that I visit each cell in the morning running errands. It's true. Nobody has even dared ask me to deliver so much as an illicit message. I'm not going to be a carrier pigeon, there's no way. But how do the guards know that?

They don't know. But they trust Ariel.

Everybody trusts Ariel. He's the one that connects all the characters. And *The Tempest* has united all of us. Those of us in the theatre company go off to one side during the exercise hour to talk about our parts. We address each other as Antonio, Gonzalo, Ferdinand...the one who's worst off in this respect is Trinculo, because it sounds kind of rude in Italian, but even he prefers to go by his stage name. The fact is we've all come to the same realisation: now that we know these new characters, we can never go back to being who we were before. They're all grander than we are. All of them, even the worst ones. Even Antonio, who wants to kill his brother. He is part of this strange kind of magic, one that allows us to stand on stage and do something nobody can ever do in real life. And it helps us understand something that we've never understood in real life.

Sometimes it wasn't easy. After the performance of *Napoli milionaria*, some of the other inmates took a nasty turn. They're still criminals, and certainly not theatre types. All they saw that night was Sasà in a skirt. They tried to make fun of me: 'Donna Amalia, you gonna bring me a coffee?'

I had to throw a couple of them against the wall.

'You'll find Donna Amalia in the theatre. But here, I'm Sasà. Got it?' Whether I'm on stage or off, I'm still a Hothead—that's the message. I'm certainly not a man who'll just stand there and be made fun of.

But now that we're rehearsing *The Tempest*, even those guys are beginning to show a little more respect. They can see that this thing is drawing interest from newspapers and television channels—a couple of journalists have even come to sit in on rehearsals—and we're starting to become a source of pride. They can see that we're changing, that we're coming together. Of course, they tell us off because we try to avoid strikes and disputes with prison management: we don't want to risk having the project shut down. But they understand that it's thanks to theatre that we've been able to find a way to communicate, to reduce the distance between inmates and guards, and change their attitude towards us. And this is good for everybody, including them.

One day the warden comes to talk to us. He wants to hear how the show is going and what progress we're making. We explain the plot and characters, getting pretty animated.

'And then there's Ferdinand, poor guy, he's in love but he thinks he's not going to be able to marry the girl he loves...'

'And what about Gonzalo's monologue? How great is that? *I'th' commonwealth I would by contraries execute all things.*'

'Nah, but the best of the lot is Trinculo, that bit where he decides he's going to be king of the island...' The two drunks that nobody wanted to play have now become the most popular characters.

An hour and a half into our meeting, we realise that the warden, who spoke at the beginning, has now been silent for some time.

'So, what do you think?' I ask him. He looks a bit dazed. Maybe he doesn't like us.

'I...Do you realise you haven't talked at all about prison?'

'Prison? What's prison got to do with it?'

'In my twenty-year career,' he says slowly, 'I've not once spent an hour and a half chatting to prisoners without speaking at all about prison. I've not once spent this long talking about the theatre.'

Huh, it's true. This statement knocks us out. How many days has it been since I talked about prison, about the problems in here? How many weeks has it been since I gave it any thought? How many nights not turning towards the wall in shame, holding back the tears, thinking that the darkness will never end?

'You know, sir,' I say, shaking my head, unable to keep a smile from my lips. 'You need to get out more.'

'Thanks, Sasà. You write real beautiful.' Lello steps away, putting the sheet of paper in his pocket and glancing around to check if anybody has seen him. But even if they have, nobody will say anything. At least twenty of the guys in here get me to write their love letters for them.

As soon as you take up reading, you're faced with a problem: you suddenly know loads more words. And if you read poetry, it's even worse: you know more beautiful words. Words for love, regret, tenderness, longing—feelings that no one in here is capable of expressing. Leafing through the pages of all those books, I found myself with my hands full of words. And I wouldn't be Ariel if I didn't decide to throw them all up into the air and let them float onto the dry pages of these men's letters, these men who have never been granted words.

> *I love thee best when joy has fled*
> *thy cowering brow and eyes aghast;*
> *when all thy heart is drowned in dread;*
> *when life for thee is overspread*
> *by dreadful storm-clouds from the past.*

Thou cam'st to kindle, goest to come; then I
Will dream that hope again, but else would die.

From the way these poets are able to describe love and absence, you'd think they were all condemned to weekly prison visits. One by one, following the recommendations of don Pasquale, who knows heaps about poetry, I've been accompanied from the library back to my cell by the lot of them: Baudelaire and Neruda, Donne and Quevedo. But the best, the greatest, remains Shakespeare.

I soon discovered that, as well as theatre, he wrote a lot of sonnets, and I can't drag myself away from the music I hear in them. Even the other inmates have learned where the most beautiful love poetry comes from, and when I write their letters they ask, 'Can you stick some of that Shapesgear in?' I remember that not so long ago I was mangling that name, too, and it's hard to believe. They ask cautiously for Shakespeare, as though they were asking for a prohibited drug, and I write their wives addictive words.

Save that my soul's imaginary sight
Presents thy shadow to my sightless view,
Which like a jewel hung in ghastly night
Makes black night beauteous, and her old face new.

Let me not to the marriage of true minds
Admit impediments; love is not love
Which alters when it alterations finds,
Or bends with the remover to remove.

If I could write the beauty of your eyes,
And in fresh numbers number all your graces.

Shall I compare thee to a summer's day?
Thou art more lovely and more temperate.

Yet do thy worst, old Time, despite thy wrong,
My love shall in my verse ever live young.

Once I've handed over the umpteenth letter, I go back to my cell feeling a little melancholy. Writing for other people's women makes me miss Monica more than ever. I open up a collection by Baudelaire that I haven't yet returned, and perhaps never will, because some days I find my very own torment in those pages, and because so many verses are about the sea. The sea that I miss so much.

love Ocean always, Man: ye both are free!
the Sea, thy mirror: thou canst find thy soul
in the unfurling billows' surging roll,
thy mind's abyss is bitter as the sea.

Things are not looking good if I find myself agreeing with Baudelaire. 'And poets tire of verse and maids of love.' Maybe I'm just tired of writing other people's letters. But what if Monica's tired of loving me? What if she's tired of coming to see me every two weeks, married to a kind of ghost that she can't even touch? What if she's tired of waiting for me?

What if she's no longer my Miranda?

To a prisoner, Miranda is the ideal woman. Chaste, perfect; he dreams his woman on the outside is like this, too, but knows she's not. Like everyone else, I spend ages trying not to think that my wife could be cheating on me—a lot of us are on medication just to keep that particular thought at bay. We know that if things were the other way around, we would never wait ten years for our wife. Not even eight years, or five. It's not how men are made. It's in our nature to cheat. Women cheat out of spite, lack of affection, revenge, or because they lose their way. Women cheat because of absence. Absence...

But Monica is like Miranda. The woman who says, 'Girls, when you feel like your heart is going to stop, then that's it—forget about your head, don't go flitting about.' Miranda is faithful to Ferdinand from the very first day. And when her father tells her that she can't love Ferdinand, because she's never seen any other man apart from Caliban, she replies: 'My affections are then most humble. I have no ambition to see a goodlier man'. It's love. And she's the love we all wish for.

Monica is Miranda, I'm sure of it. But I'm no Ferdinand. None of us is. Ferdinand helps carry her load and takes away her troubles, whereas we've never saved our wives any toil. I went out stealing, and all I brought home was stolen bread, too meagre to nourish the soul. Stolen bread doesn't satisfy. In fact, it makes you even hungrier because you swallow guilt along with it. And the person who receives it is unable to eat peacefully, either. I remember those evenings as I lay next to Monica, after we made love, when she would say bitterly: 'I bet as soon as it gets dark you'll run off to use cocaine; you prefer it to my company. What do you want from me?'

I'd like to have been Ferdinand, or even to become him. To know how to be close to the person you love, to make a simple gesture that's not the usual ritual of flowers and gifts. So perhaps it's not by chance that at this very moment, my eyes fall on the little mirror in my cell.

I stand up and detach it from the wall. I take some salt and lemon juice and I scrub hard with a rag until the white enamel on the back comes off. This way the mirror becomes a sheet you can see through; another inmate taught me this.

Then I go and get a photo of Monica, a close-up in which she looks especially beautiful. I like it a lot and it's hard to part with it, but Ferdinand is guiding me. Carefully, I attach the photo to the mirror, along with a smaller photo of a rose. Now, when I look into it I see Monica, as beautiful as a painting.

Satisfied, I step back and look at my handiwork. I realise it's the first time I've really, with my own hands, made something for her.

When I hand it to her the next day during her visit, she gets pissed off.

'What'd you do that for? Who'd you give my photo to? One of those jerk-off friends of yours—who knows what he did with it before sticking it here?'

She can't believe that I made it myself. Better not tell her I had help from Ferdinand—she'll think it's the name of some lifer.

'Are you dumb?' is all I say in protest. 'I only ever look at your photos at night, so that nobody else sees them!'

She's always been able to tell when I'm lying, so she sees now that I'm telling the truth. The expression on her face is one of disbelief.

'You made it? Really? What brought that on?'

'Don't you like it?' I ask, a little disappointed.

'Of course I like it! I like it a lot!' And she bursts into tears.

'Oh God, Monica…don't cry…' I don't know where to look now. I'm pleased that she's touched, but who knows what Gaetano will think. He's over in the corner. His wife cries all the time, but it's because she wants to leave him. 'I didn't want to make you cry…'

'No, no, it's just that it's such a beautiful thing…but…you're not you anymore.' She looks at me, her eyes a mix of tears and astonishment.

She's right. I'm no longer me. But, at the same time, I'm more myself than ever before. I'm still Sasà, but now I'm also Ariel, and Ferdinand, too. All I can say is, 'It's because this theatre thing is doing me good.'

'You're turning this Shakespeare thing into an obsession…'

Women. They worry when you're doing badly, they worry when you're doing well, if you're doing the right thing, or the wrong thing…I shake my head, trying not to get emotional myself, otherwise this will start looking like a Greek tragedy, and I'm not a fan of those.

I try to explain. 'It's because he…Shakespeare…tells me the story of my own life. He allows me to make his words my own, to say them in my own way. He's in my head because what he wrote, you see, is true for everybody.'

'As long as you're feeling good…' she says shyly, still not quite understanding. 'And as long as you keep making beautiful things like this!' She points to the mirror with her photo and finally smiles, my Miranda.

Maybe it's true, I think, as I go back to my cell. Maybe I am turning it into an obsession. But with all this metaphor business, Shakespeare really opens up your mind. The stuff he writes, the situations and characters he creates—they're not only true in that one situation. He's constantly renewing himself, so he never gets old. Thanks to Shakespeare and Ariel, I've begun to understand my life, and to read it differently from before.

Before now, quite simply, I hadn't read the script properly. Thanks to him, I've learned that the world is not chaotic, I just never knew how to interpret it. That's the greatest tip an artist could ever receive.

But am I an artist?

9

'Pardon, master,
I will be correspondent to command
And do my spiriting gently.'

Ariel in *The Tempest*
Act I, Scene II

'Prospero's not that harsh in this scene!' I can't take it anymore.
This time it's coming straight from the heart. When Cosimo
turns around to look at me, his eyes are already spitting flames.

'I'm sorry?'

'No, *I'm* sorry, Cosimo.' We've been rehearsing together for
months but I'm still deferential towards him. I know he prefers
it that way. 'But the thing is, over the course of the play, Prospero
changes emotionally. He starts out being very harsh, and goes
all the way through to granting forgiveness...' Cosimo might be
the lead actor and head of the company, but his Prospero keeps

the same level of rage from beginning to end. He doesn't grow, he doesn't change and he's not convincing.

'What a load of nonsense!' he snorts. 'Prospero's a harsh man, bitter…'

'He is at the beginning,' I say, nodding. 'But then he finds peace. At the end he weighs it all up, delivers his judgments, and puts everything right. He grants the dukedom to his son-in-law, along with his daughter, because they're the next generation, he forgives his brother, he forgives everybody, and he says to the good Gonzalo: "noble friend, you helped me, I respect and value you."'

I look across at Proietti, who squares his shoulders proudly. He's perfect as Gonzalo. A man in his sixties who fully embodies his role, who truly believes in it. His hair is completely white and when he acts his bright blue eyes become tinged with red because he's close to tears. He always gets emotional, and he's right to, because his character has one of the most beautiful monologues in anything I've read so far by Shakespeare, and by now I've read a great deal.

'You want to teach me how to play my character, but you haven't understood a thing,' Cosimo cuts me off disdainfully. 'Prospero accepts the situation, but he doesn't forgive those who betrayed him. And they were the very people who were closest to him, too.'

I'm guessing in his past Cosimo must have been betrayed by some real *infami*.

'Well, obviously…people who don't know you can't really

hurt you, can they?' I point out. 'You'd have to be really unlucky to get betrayed by someone who doesn't even know you.'

'That doesn't justify it!' Cosimo protests. 'It's the disappointment over the betrayal that explains Prospero's rage.'

'But what you're taking on stage isn't Prospero's rage,' I say, even though I know I shouldn't. 'It's Cosimo's rage.'

He purses his lips and I can see that he's absolutely furious, like he's never been before. This is where all his accumulated frustrations really emerge. I know he'd like to throw me out, but he can't, and this makes him even angrier.

'This discussion is really interesting,' says Cavalli, stepping in before things turn ugly. 'But let's start back up again. It was going well.'

I keep quiet, but I'm not entirely grateful to him for intervening. I'm not the kind of person who'll never change his opinion, but nor am I someone who's happy to keep his mouth shut. I'd really like to resolve this Prospero business. I don't like the way Cosimo plays him: so harsh, bitter and unmoving. I feel like he's taking something away, a lot away in fact, from the greatness of the character Shakespeare created.

I don't see Prospero as a negative character. He's not a cop, who weighs everything up and then delivers your sentence. He makes a point of promising Ariel freedom and giving his blessing to his daughter's wedding, but chooses not to eliminate the men who twice tried to kill him. He works on them through the heart, showing by example. He basically says to his brother, 'I do not despise you; you should despise yourself.' His punishment is to make his brother ashamed of himself, simply by telling him what a wicked *infame* he was. A voice can do more harm than the sword: to do good requires deeds, but true vengeance comes through words. Words can wound more, yet leave the body intact. They cause damage on the inside, not on the outside, but with that damage they can heal. This is exactly the message Shakespeare sends with Prospero: when you find yourselves in truly serious difficulty, talk to one another, discuss it, use the word as an instrument, ultimately, for healing hatred. This is the true magic of Prospero: turning vendetta into justice.

But how can you convey that message if Prospero stays enraged right to the end? If the acting doesn't show his great act of forgiveness?

I'm not going to keep quiet.

'Prospero is a man of his word,' I start up again, determined. I see Cavalli signalling for me to be quiet from behind Cosimo's back. I see Cosimo stiffen; he's already offended. I don't care. These guys haven't understood Prospero. It's up to me to defend him. Since I've already put my foot in it, I decide to go all the way. I get up on the highest bunk bed, the one Ariel often jumps and speaks from. 'Prospero is a man of mercy. In the end, who else shows forgiveness? Only Prospero. What is it that's harsh about this man? What was he supposed to do? Is it his discipline that you've got a problem with?' I ask mournfully. All the others are looking up at me.

'It doesn't hurt to be a little harsh in this perverted world, where no one respects anyone anymore. Prospero absolves everybody in the end, forgives them all, reconciles them and even helps two people come together, one of whom is his only daughter, so that a new generation can begin...Who has that sort of ability nowadays? Where are the great men? Where are the Prosperos? Send someone out to find them, because we sure need them...There are no longer any masters. Or, perhaps, we all want to be masters, but nobody wants to do the hard yards.'

They have to understand that Prospero is not a harsh man for the sake of it, but out of a sense of responsibility. He's harsh because he sees that human beings are undisciplined. Prospero comes up close and he says to you: 'You're a false and insolent swindler, but you should be living a pure, honest life.' He says: 'You can't do that, how dare you?' We should have more school principals like Prospero. We could do with a Prospero in Naples. We should welcome figures with this kind of harshness, but alongside it, a sense of justice.

'Think about it for a moment. Prospero even saves Caliban and turns him good. In this way he shows that if you want to do a good deed, you can transform even the very worst material. Like Ariel, Caliban is a servant, but while Ariel is a good spirit—and Prospero is harsh with him because he's too naïve and he has so much to learn—Caliban is an animal. And yet he doesn't eliminate him. If there's one quality Prospero has above all others, it is a love of life, and of love itself. He shows it in the way he allows his daughter to share with Ferdinand everything that Prospero never got to share with his own wife, and through that act he restores everything to the way it ought to be. He's not capable of hatred. He has the capacity to govern, but in such an evil world he can't do it, because everybody is attached to power, apart from him. It's no surprise that he's enraged. He's been betrayed not once, but twice…yet in spite of it all, he doesn't line the traitors up for execution, like he could. No, he uses a new language: a language of forgiveness. This is the strongest element of all, stronger even than revenge. As strong as freedom.'

On the word 'freedom', my voice catches in my throat. I've yet been able to come to an agreement with freedom.

I look down at all the astonished faces and I realise I've given a monologue of my own, as though I fancy myself some kind of Shakespeare. I also realise that Cosimo is never going to forgive me.

I jump down off the bed and run to Gaetano and tell him I'm unwell. I ask him to take me back to my cell or get another guard to take me back. I'm in too much of a mess to stick around. He can tell I'm upset and I manage to get taken to my cell. The whole way back, Prospero's exchange with Ariel keeps pounding through my head.

> *How now? Moody? What is't thou canst demand?*
> *My liberty.*
> *Before the time be out? No more!*

I had trouble with Prospero to begin with, but in rehearsal I learned to accept that I have to serve him to gain my freedom. The fact is, though, when you're in prison, talk of freedom hurts. A lot.

I *am* Ariel. I messed up and I lost my liberty, both physical and emotional. If I mess up again, I'm not getting out. Prospero warns me, tells me what not to do, if I don't want to make things worse without realising it. And if I accuse him of behaving unjustly because he hasn't yet given me my freedom, he attacks me, and rightly so. Have I forgotten how things used to be? I was imprisoned in a tree, imprisoned in my own story. He gave me another story. And now I'm complaining? I deserve to go back into that tree if I can't appreciate what I've received.

And I do appreciate it, truly, I think, pacing up and down in my cell. I'm not like Prospero. I can't always be just and reasonable. I've taken a lot of short cuts in life, and not by chance.

In the evening I visit don Pasquale. I need to talk to him. Just seeing him go through the motions of making coffee calms me down. It's like a ritual.

'I had an argument with Cosimo.'

'With Cosimo? How come? Did he order you about too much?'

Don Pasquale knows me so well. The only person I take orders from is my mother.

'Not this time. In fact, I ordered *him* about too much.' And I explain what happened.

When I've finished speaking he sits down in front of me with an intense look on his face, unlike any I've seen before.

'Sasà,' he says in a serious tone, 'why is this business with Prospero having such an effect on you?'

'I told you! Because Cosimo just doesn't get Prospero, he

doesn't know how to play him and—'

'There are other actors in the group who aren't playing their characters well,' he gently reminds me.

'But he should be able to. He's the head of the company!'

'The problem is not that he doesn't know how to act,' he replies, not letting up. 'It's that he doesn't know how to play *Prospero*.'

'Yes. And that's no small thing.'

'Maybe,' he says, nodding. 'But it still doesn't explain why you're getting so worked up.'

'Because…because I don't like seeing an injustice done to Prospero.'

'You don't like seeing an injustice done to Prospero…' Don Pasquale's eyes narrow. He's a falcon about to swoop down on his prey. '…Or to your father?'

He's gone straight for my heart. Those dark eyes of his capture me and I feel myself whirling and plummeting into a well, where all my memories are held. When I was nine years old, my mother was the woman in my life; I wanted to marry someone exactly like her. And my father was a hero, next to whom I ought only to have felt ashamed, even at that age.

I didn't belong to his stock: they were all good people, hardworking, incapable of malice or dishonesty. I was the alien, the black sheep. Worse—I was patchy and stained, ugly and mangy. I had never done anything to be worthy of his name—and perhaps never would.

My father could never understand why we did all that

stuff—cutting cocaine, even in the house, carrying weapons—
he just couldn't understand. And I couldn't understand him.

'What's the point of going to the docks at five-thirty every
morning to unload a ship, just so you can come home at the end
of the day too worn out even to lift a spoon from your bowl to
your mouth?' I used to sneer.

It was only later that I understood. After the turf war and
the crisis, when I had to go into exile in Spain. That was when
I understood that I'd taken after my mother in every way.
She taught me to love my friends but respect my enemies. She
taught me to fight, and to survive. Whereas my father, a man
of few words and many actions, tried until his dying breath,
but never taught me anything. Or maybe he taught me values
I didn't realise I'd learned until I met Prospero: patience and
justice.

Prospero who turns everything upside down, who turns
black into white. Prospero who, after so many years, placed
a hand on my head and said to do what I was told and 'thou
shalt ere long be free'. Prospero who helped me understand
how I should behave when I recognise love, whether my own or
witnessed. How to respect it, how to observe it. Prospero who
explained that you should never take revenge, not under any
circumstances, because it will never fill you up, in fact it empties
you out, because it even takes from you the victim, the person
you'd attacked in the hope you might hate yourself a little less.
Prospero who showed me that it is wiser to humiliate than to
eliminate, that cold revenge just means killing yourself day after

day, until you turn around and say, 'Enough, I understand how I should behave.'

No wonder I got pissed off when I heard Prospero being denigrated.

'Don Pasquale, you're a genius.' It's only when I speak, that I realise I'm sobbing.

'Not at all. I'm a failure.' He's choked up, too, and he looks at me as though I'm his son.

'Don't say that.' I'm alarmed by the desperation in his voice. All this time locked up inside himself is not healthy. I've been aware of that for a while. The counsellors try to get him leave permits but he says to give them to someone else. He's crushed. He's let himself get fucked over by prison and now that I'm seeing him in tears for the first time, I have confirmation of this. He's in exile inside his cell, on his island, but he's too weak to summon up a tempest.

'I don't have the strength anymore. Maybe I'll end it all,' he murmurs.

'You don't mean you want to kill yourself?' The shock stops my crying and takes away my manners. But he doesn't take offence at my brutal question.

'I have nothing to do in this world,' he says in reply.

'But why? Don't you know how many people out there love you and need you?'

I'm Ariel, trying to fix everything, but I have before me a broken Prospero. Between the two of us we don't have enough certainties to get through a single evening.

All we can do is hug in silence.

In here, you can't do anything for anybody else, I think, as I feel his tears on my neck. Unlike Prospero, don Pasquale can neither give nor take forgiveness.

What about me? Can I forgive, or be forgiven?

'You're contagious.' The section head has an unfriendly look on her face. And yet I haven't proposed anything bad. 'You make lifers cry, you get the guards dancing in the corridors...' They must have told her about yesterday, when I was washing the floors, and practised in front of Gaetano a few of the leaps I plan to do on stage as Ariel. Damn CCTV cameras. 'And now this. Doing theatre is bad for you. You're dreaming too much.'

On this point, she's probably right. Is it possible to dream too much? It seems like a good idea to me, and it's clear by now that I'm not someone who gives up easily on a good idea.

'What's wrong with the idea, ma'am? We want to get things tidied up. It's gross down there. It's ugly and we get hurt playing football. Maybe we could even grow vegetables.'

Needless to say, the idea came to me thanks to a line in *The Tempest*, when I go to tell Prospero the parts of the island where the shipwreck victims have wound up.

'The king's son have I landed by himself; whom I left cooling of the air with sighs in an odd angle of the isle and sitting, his arms in this sad knot,' says Ariel, who has treated the young prince Ferdinand with the utmost respect. This line always makes me sad. It reminds me that I was born a hundred and fifty metres from the sea, and I miss it desperately. I picture Ferdinand sitting on a bed of aromatic seaside grass. I've never seen anything like that before, though, so I went to the library and got Bennett to give me a big book with drawings and descriptions of flowers and plants. While I was flicking through it, I got the idea.

'Guys, how about we make a garden?'

'A garden, where?' At first, the other actors were sceptical.

'Down in the yard, where we have our exercise hour.' The space we use for the exercise hour is just a patch of dry ground with a few weeds, as barren as a war zone. On one side there are the cells of prisoners who have been given extra punishment, on the other side there's a covered area for hanging out washing, and beyond that the cement area where we play football. It's a space that could make a whole troupe of clowns miserable.

Several of us belong to an environmental group, where we do what we can with a donation of ten euros a month from prison. Those who have leave permits sometimes clean up public parks and piazzas when they're on the outside. So why not turn our hellish yard into the garden of Eden, to put it in a way Dante might like? What's more logical than that?

So off I went to ask the section head.

'Striano, leaving aside the fact that you have a hundred ideas for each one you actually follow through on, I'd be happy to allow this. It would be nice, and it would be something I'd feel proud of,' she tells me. She has the tone of voice of a person explaining something that ought to be obvious even to an idiot.

'But you're maximum-security prisoners. How can I allow you to have picks, shovels…'

I hadn't even thought of that. It's true: what might be simple garden tools on the outside take on a whole other appearance in a place where even a belt is considered a weapon…And how can you do gardening without digging, without breaking up the soil?

'But we wouldn't use them as weapons! We're normal people!' I try to protest.

'Striano, you're really not all that normal.'

I look around the office in search of inspiration, praying to Shakespeare for a brilliant idea. Then my eyes fall on the coffee maker.

'Ma'am, if I wanted to, I could kill you with that coffee maker,' I say.

'Excuse me?' She doesn't leap back. This line of work gives you strong nerves.

'I bash you on the head with it nine or ten times until you die,' I calmly explain. 'Or, look, I could kill you with a blade. I run behind the desk, grab you like this and cut your throat.' I demonstrate the action. She stiffens. She glances across at the guard.

'I don't have a blade, ma'am,' I hasten to add, before she gets me thrown into solitary—that's the last thing I need with rehearsal tomorrow. 'I was just making a point. That if I want to kill, I can kill. And so can the others.'

'Striano, don't frighten me.'

'Frighten you? The point is, ma'am, we *don't* want to kill.'

She nods to the guard, who is standing behind me.

'Did you hear him? He's going through the thousand ways he wants to kill me.'

'Ma'am, nobody wants to kill you. But let us do this,' I insist.

There is a heavy silence in the room as she looks at me and reflects. I know I haven't convinced her. She's thinking about the right way to say no kindly.

'What if I'm with them?' It's the guard speaking. I turn in astonishment.

'In what sense?' the section head asks.

'The picks and shovels…If we let them have them, but I'm standing right there armed, what can they do?'

Thank you, spirit of Shakespeare, I think. *You inspired the guard!*

The section head stares at her subordinate as if to say: 'Whose side are you on, anyway?' But I can see she's trying not to laugh. She's my age, and we get on well.

'All right then,' she sighs deeply, partly in exasperation and partly in amusement. 'Let's fill out some forms and send off an application. I'm not promising anything, Striano. The warden will be the one to decide, okay?'

She calls me back two days later.

'Striano, I'm to inform you that the warden is enthusiastic about your project. And he's approved it.'

And so it is that five of us—two Romans, an Apulian, a Calabrian and I—meet up in the middle of the yard. At first we feel despair. The garden space, which is minuscule when crowded with inmates, now seems vast. It all needs digging over.

'We have to till the soil,' says one of the Romans, who knows his stuff. So of course he starts studying the area and different seed types, while the rest of us break our backs with spades and picks. But I don't mind hard work, or at least, I don't mind this kind of work. I feel like we're creating something.

We plant tomatoes, eggplant and capsicum, thinking that maybe others will harvest them after us. In prison, you think of the long term, and you do things for those who'll be coming in further down the track. In the big clearing we plant grass and with two rows of stones we mark off a little path that winds through the field to reach the other area. We line it with roses, which we'll be able to pick for our wives. We plant bulbs— strange things that look dead as stones but will become the most colourful flowers of all.

As I turn over the soil I see it regain life and I'm already thinking of the splendour that will one day transform this abandoned patch of earth. Just like in the theatre, we're not interested in doing an amateur job. We're no dilettantes. We want a garden as beautiful, if not more so, than the gardens on the outside. We want to measure up to that standard…Of course, it's the same old story—we're a bunch of swaggering *guappi* and this damn attitude of ours is exactly what got us into trouble in the first place. But you can't simply get rid of that kind of attitude in people. You just have to give them a chance to use it positively rather than negatively. For example, through gardening instead of dealing.

As my sweat drips into the soil I start reciting lines. Gonzalo's monologue, the speech that is almost a promise:

I'th' commonwealth I would by contraries
Execute all things, for no kind of traffic
Would I admit; no name of magistrate;
Letters should not be known; riches, poverty
And use of service, none; contract, succession,
Bourn, bound of land, tilth, vineyard—none;
No use of metal, corn, or wine or oil;
No occupation, all men idle, all;
And women, too, but innocent and pure;
No sovereignty—
[…]
All things in common nature should produce
Without sweat or endeavour: treason, felony,
Sword, pike, knife, gun, or need of any engine,
Would I not have; but nature should bring forth
Of its own kind all foison, all abundance,
To feed my innocent people.

INTERMEZZO

Ever wondered why prison screws you over? Because, bit by bit, you start to feel like you're owed something. They don't know how to rehabilitate you, they don't know how to reskill you, they don't know what the fuck to do with you. You move from a situation of debt, as you've committed a crime and have a debt to society, to one of credit, as you have to battle to be granted the rights you're owed.

Ladies and gentlemen, you shouldn't make us feel like we're owed something. You should help us understand our own story, understand where things went wrong, where we lost our way. And not just understand where one individual prisoner went wrong, but where we as a society went wrong. Having a story is like having a direction. That's why theatre is therapeutic: it tells you how not to degenerate, where not to go.

It's not just theatre. It's books, too. When Prospero finds himself all alone with his little daughter, exiled to an island by the wickedness of men and also perhaps by his own mistakes, he doesn't let himself be overcome. Why? Not only because he is a great master, but also because he has books to keep him company. Books are humankind's memories; they're like men who can no longer hurt you. Within them, in distilled form, lies all the goodness of the humanity that left them behind. All you need is to encounter books, and choose well in what you take from them.

You can attain anything from books. Any light, any mission. Easily. On the streets it's hard to find goodness. It's hidden under piles of stupid, useless, dangerous stuff. In books, the good stuff is right on top. It emerges, alive, from the words and from the pages because, when people write, unlike when they live their lives, they are able to stop and reflect. People almost never do that in everyday life, and this is how they cause trouble.

You see, we're all in debt—to ourselves, to our neighbour, to life. In books we can find wealth, maybe not enough to pay off this debt, but enough to reduce it, to be able to manage it. That's why I say, instead of setting your alarm for seven in the morning, set it for quarter to seven, and try reading for fifteen minutes.

Then, maybe, you'll cause less trouble out in the world.

PART FOUR
'GIVE ME MY FREEDOM'

'You would play upon me, you would seem to know my stops, you would pluck out the heart of my mystery, you would sound me from my lowest note to the top of my compass; and there is much music, excellent voice, in this little organ, yet cannot you make it speak.'

Hamlet in *Hamlet*
Act III, Scene II

10

'The dram of evil
Doth all the noble substance often dout
To his own scandal.'

Hamlet in *Hamlet*
Act I, Scene IV

'Carminati said to tell you, nice work.'

I look up from examining the meat, which this time isn't green. It might seem obvious that meat wouldn't be green, but in prison you can't be so sure. The prison catering contract isn't just about feeding the inmates. It's a business. And let's just say that quality is not always guaranteed. So we convinced the guards to allow some of us to be present at food deliveries, to do quality control.

They wouldn't have granted us permission for this if it hadn't been for the theatre project. Ever since we founded the Company of Free Asocial Artists—that's what we call ourselves—things have changed. Even the guards' periodic inspections of our cells have become less disrespectful and destructive. The warden trusts us now. We've given him our guarantee that there will be no mobile phones, drugs or weapons. They, in turn, will respect the little things that help us maintain some dignity in this grey world: the shelves we build out of cigarette-packet papier-mâché, the little curtains we put up in our cells for a little privacy...

'I care for you all and I've never treated you like prisoners,' the warden likes to remind us. It's true. And here we are, checking that the meat's not green, the spinach yellow, or the tomatoes brown.

In this job you also get to meet prisoners from other blocks. It's our only point of contact with inmates who aren't in maximum security. Today, it's a couple of white-collar prisoners taking the delivery. These are guys with privileges, militants who are in for political activities. They're from section G8.

In Rebibbia, section G8 is the central area, where they keep the inmates who are ready for rehabilitation. For those of us who are in for a different kind of crime, and who are in many cases considered dangerous, G8 is the finishing line we long to reach. It's the last stage before release. And because they're all a bit freer over in section G8, it is also the centre of the prison's socio-cultural world: bands, theatre, drawing, painting.

I knew it was only a matter of time before the regular inmates saw us on the news or read about us in the paper, and began to wonder: 'Hey, what's this theatre group doing in maximum security? Why aren't we running this?'

They're the intellectuals, while we're the wild animals. How did we manage to start a theatre company capable of attracting media attention? If there's a certain actor in Rebibbia who the newspapers say is better than those on the outside (in all modesty), how is it possible he's not one of theirs?

So here they are, sniffing around.

The problem is that we can't stand the guys from section G8.

'Carminati sends his regards,' the tall, bald guy tries again, since I didn't reply the first time but kept on working.

'What's Carminati got to do with us?' I ask, looking up at him from the case of tomatoes.

'He heard about the theatre project and says he can help you,' he replies.

'Help us how?' I ask in a flat tone. The tomatoes are showing more expression than my face right now, I don't want to let on that the rage is starting to bubble up inside me. Go on, say it. You want to take over the group for your own purposes. Do you think we were born yesterday?

How dare they, I think, furious. *How fucking dare they?*

'Well, I'll let him know I passed on the message. Maybe he'll write you a note,' the bald guy says, retreating. I guess my face wasn't so expressionless after all.

I know it seems absurd but ours is a respectable section of the prison. The Calabrians don't even like it if we go out without a T-shirt on during the exercise hour. It offends their sensibility. We've had to create a separate section that we call

'Nudists' Walk', where you can hang out in shorts and a singlet on the days when the heat is deadly. Otherwise it's long trousers and, at best, short-sleeved shirts. And, since the theatre project's been up and running, there has not been a single brawl, not a single breach. We've become model prisoners. And now *we're* supposed to wheel and deal with these political militants?

The following week at food delivery inspection time, it's not the bald guy I encounter, but Carminati himself. He heads straight for me—not that I was under the illusion he was there to accompany the spinach.

'Do you know who I am?' he asks, addressing me politely. He really makes an impression, I can't deny it. There is a hard look in his eye and in his demeanour the infinite arrogance of a man who is used to being obeyed, even by the powerful, and even from inside a prison.

'No, I don't know who you are,' I say out of contempt. I know perfectly well who he is, and he knows it.

'I'm Massimo Carminati,' he says regardless. He then makes a point of specifying: 'I'm not in here for the kinds of crimes you are. I'm a political prisoner.'

I weigh up a dozen different responses. From the first one that comes to mind: 'Political, my arse', to one Shakespeare might come out with: 'There's small choice in rotten apples'.

'What do I care,' is all I say. He stiffens visibly and because I don't want a fight, I quickly continue. 'If it's about the theatre group, don't talk to me, talk to Cosimo. He's head of the company.'

'Cosimo's not head of anything. He hasn't studied like I have. I can help you guys improve,' he says, with the dangerous calm of a snake.

'Maybe. But Cosimo's the one you have to convince.' I shrug. 'And I imagine that could be difficult for a right-wing militant like you. Cosimo is a leftist through and through.'

'Don't worry, I'll send him a letter. He has to do what I say.' His tone is sinister, and he cuts the conversation off there.

If he's bothered to come and speak to me in person, it means he's serious. He's worked out that something important is happening—he's no fool—and he wants to take over the company. He's not without power, either: we have no way of knowing how many prison activities are in his hands.

At rehearsal that afternoon I pose the problem to the group. I address the head of the company directly.

'Listen, Cosimo, you've got a nasty enemy in here,' I say.

'Who's that, then? I've got loads.'

'Carminati.'

A smile spreads across his lips.

'I want that guy as my enemy with all my heart.'

'Are you sure? He'll be your enemy *and* the whole company's enemy, if we turn down his help,' I remind him. I'm in complete agreement but the others need to be, too. In case there's trouble.

Cosimo looks around the room.

'Does anyone here want to accept Carminati's help? Does anyone want to let him join the company?' he asks.

The thick chorus of 'No!' makes Gaetano jump; he's

standing guard in the usual spot near the door.

'We don't want his sort!'

'They're not worthy of being involved! It's our company!'

Who'd have thought these men would bring me such satis-faction? I already knew we weren't a bunch of sissies—after all, it's not like we're in here for stealing lollies from children—but seeing such a united front against an aggressor is a whole other thing, and it fills me with pride.

We don't want his sort. Firstly, because they stole indiscrim-inately from everybody—on the outside, in here, everywhere. And secondly, because they're militants—they are truly evil people. If I've got a score to settle with you, I'll come and see you and—maybe—I'll kill you, but I won't go planting a bomb in the piazza to kill you, taking out fifty innocent bystanders, too. We're all lawbreakers, but they didn't just succumb to the undeniable appeal of being an outlaw, they had the sinister determination of the criminal. The politics of bombings disgusts us. And when someone responsible for that sort of crime acci-dentally ends up in a cell with us, it takes less than forty-eight hours for him to realise he'd be better off with a change of scene. He ends up going to the guards himself and saying, 'Send me away cause this lot'll kill me.'

And now they'd like to help us? They want to run the company? Oh, *please!* I exchange glances with Cosimo.

'So I should decline Carminati's kind offer?' I ask, all refined, with a little sneer for the benefit of our band of rebels. I'm only asking so I can hear them roar their assent. We truly are a team.

Just for an instant, I see myself back in the Quartieri, with the Hotheads. Once again, I feel the heat of our unity in victory and in danger, the strong connection that comes from a sense of belonging, that tight-knit quality that makes the group even stronger when facing an enemy. But back then it was something nasty uniting us: trafficking, violence, the dangerous fervour of cocaine. Now it's the pure spirit of theatre. Now we're invincible.

And we're supposed to put ourselves in the hands of someone else? Someone who'll manage us however he likes, and could screw us over any moment? No way. We'll show him.

I'm all fired up like a victor in battle who fought off the enemy. I realise my blood hasn't flowed this fast in my veins for many, many months.

And that very night I find I have company.

For some reason I wake up in the dead of the night. Perhaps a premonition has put me on alert, or there is some movement in the shadows of my cell. It's the hour before dawn, when ghosts roam freely through the dark. And there he is, leaning against the wall. He has long, wavy brown hair, with a crown resting on top. His regal robes are dirty, as though they've been spattered with mud. He's cleaning under his fingernail with a dagger. Then he hears me sit up in bed and he fixes his eyes on me.

'So foul and fair a day I have not seen,' he whispers.

My first thought is: *You didn't get to see too many days at all, you bastard.* My second: *Of course. I ought to have been expecting a visit from him for a while now.* He's the worst of all the bad guys.

Traitor to his friends; murderer. So arrogant, so defiant, so eager to believe the prophecies that suit him. I'm not one to laugh at suffering, but I really love it when his time comes, at the end of the play. When everything comes to a head and the moral of the tale is revealed in all its purity: sooner or later, all the evil you do in the world has repercussions. It's a strong message for someone who is in prison accounting for his past.

'Macbeth,' I hiss. 'What do you want?'

'Methought I heard a voice cry, "Sleep no more! Macbeth doth murther Sleep,"—the innocent Sleep; Sleep, that knits up the ravell'd sleave of care—'

'I was actually sleeping just fine,' I say, cutting him off. 'What are you doing here?'

'Every minute of his being thrusts against my near'st of life,' Macbeth raises his dagger, producing a flash of lightning from the small amount of light coming through the window, and I realise that it's my own rage I see before me.

This is what I know best: defiance. War.

I think back on Carminati's provocation, and my response. I hear the cries of the theatre company guys as they rally around Cosimo and me, shouting their 'no' and closing ranks against the enemy. In my mind's eye I re-watch our duel from the previous afternoon. The adrenaline comes rushing through my veins again, like a drug, or a poison.

The taste of war is in my mouth once more, with its metallic tang, as though I've run my tongue over Macbeth's bloodstained dagger. He stares at me, he's a man who has never stopped fighting. He's got the same crazed eyes that the guys in the Hotheads used to have.

'I'm going to hold up that jewellery shop,' I can hear a friend say, off in the distance, one dull afternoon that would change his life. 'Who's coming with me?'

'We don't rob people here in the Quartieri. Forget it.' My reply echoes around the room, as it did back then.

'The owner's not from the Quartieri. He's a piece of shit and we know it and we have to rob him.'

I see it all unfold, the way it was recounted to me afterwards. The friend and Rocky going into the shop, the jeweller's reaction, the gun firing, the busted knees, and then another robbery, and another…eighteen years in jail. That's what criminals are like: he could quit anytime; he's like a gambler. But instead he figures if he places another bet, he'll win again. And of course he doesn't.

I lost, too. I could have won. But I didn't know when to stop.

'Be these juggling fiends no more believed, that palter with us in a double sense.' Macbeth is following the flow of my thoughts, just as the witches read his.

Each of us has a prophecy for our own lives. The witches are those neighbours, town councillors or local bigots who warn you what will happen if you behave a certain way. And you think you can scoff at their prophecies and interpret them in your own favour. You think you can escape the consequences of what you're doing. You think you already know how it's going to be and that you hold no responsibility for what happens. But instead you're writing your own future. The script that you're following is dragging you onwards until the last bitter page, until the very end. Only you have the power to change the direction of the plot. But you don't do it.

I see myself in prison back at fourteen years of age, my first time in jail. I was on edge, as I always am when I have to read a new situation, and the counsellor, who was about twice my age, handed me a joint and she and I smoked it together. I still remember my mother's fury when she came to see me and discovered I wasn't frightened. I remember how she acted all crazy and shouted to the guards: 'Don't treat him like this. Tie him up, scare him, do something to him! He's too relaxed. It frightens me to see my son like this.' The guards laughed, but she was right. It wasn't good to be relaxed in a place like that. I should have been worried, or better, terrified. It's not normal to be in prison at fourteen years of age. If you don't realise this, then that's the road you could end up on. Like Macbeth, you might be under the illusion that you'll get away with it, and you'll go from one evil deed to the next, from one vendetta to the next. From one war to the next.

And war is a habit that's not easy to kick.

'Go away,' I tell Macbeth. He looks bewildered. He's me as I used to be. The criminal going from one mistake to the next. Why am I driving him out? Why am I renouncing myself? Have I grown tired of wars? I've never pulled back from one before.

'I'm tired of unjust wars.' I make the effort to think about

Carminati without rancour. I reason with myself, and try to understand why I should only have pity for someone like him. He sees prisoners banding together to form a united group, and he thinks only according to his own categories: he thinks we're Camorristi, Mafiosi, and that we're forming a gang to take away his power. While we are indeed strong and united, it is only in our emotion, in the joy we get from the theatre.

'We're guilty of emotional association,' I say to Macbeth, smiling, 'but unlike Mafia association, that's not yet a crime.'

A twisted grin appears on the ghost's white face, like that of a man who recognises he's been defeated. He knows he'll never be saved because he has laid out his own destiny in a jigsaw puzzle of mistakes. He never knew how to forgive himself, or how to accept forgiveness. But I do. I can be saved.

As I think about this, the ghost raises his hand in a farewell gesture.

'To-morrow, and to-morrow, and to-morrow'—the monologue I memorised so easily resounds in my head—

Creeps in this petty pace from day to day,
To the last syllable of recorded time;
And all our yesterdays have lighted fools
The way to dusty death. Out, out, brief candle!
Life's but a walking shadow; a poor player,
That struts and frets his hour upon the stage
And then is heard no more. It is a tale
Told by an idiot, full of sound and fury
Signifying nothing.

And Macbeth slowly disappears.

I lie back down with a heavy heart. Shakespeare is like that: he interrogates you, he slaps you around, he sets the world out in front of you, shining a big bright light on it that you can't ignore. And he almost chases you down in his eagerness to make you understand.

If we're going to talk about my sins, past and present, I'd have preferred to have Hamlet come and visit me. How many Hamlets have I known back in the Quartieri? How many fathers murdered, and not always by the Camorra. In Naples you don't only worry about not dying, you have to be careful *how* you die. When you're killed in a duel between two feuding gangs, there's no shortage of flowers at the cemetery: you're a god in a way you never were in life, because you died with honour. But if you're killed for being an *infame*, because of a tip-off, or the betrayal of a friend, then everyone abandons you, because slowly, the truth that cost you your life convinces even your own family that you didn't deserve to live.

You die twice. After the tragedy and the tears, after the wailing and the despair, the voice of the neighbourhood begins to tell another story, one where you're an *infame*, and that if you hadn't been a traitor you wouldn't have died. Eventually, it's not even worth the trouble of taking flowers to the cemetery for you. As a reaction to all this, your son ends up becoming another Hamlet…How many sons are there in Naples who can't decide whether or not they should avenge their father? Will they kill me, or won't they, these sons wonder.

And how many Romeos, how many Juliets? My goodness, so many! 'What do you mean you went to the movies with our enemy's daughter?' 'What the fuck do I care? You lot make me sick.' And how many Antonios, wanting to unseat a brother to grab his power, have I met in the Camorra? And then there are the women, Shakespeare's women—Macbeth's wife, Caesar's wife, Hamlet's mother. When her son confronts her about her crimes she accuses him: 'What are you on? Are you doing cocaine? Are you high? What's all this talk?' She calls her son's mental health into question, tries to feed the monsters in Hamlet's head rather than face up to her own. How many women like her have I known? Women who put the thought of war into men's heads, like the mothers and wives of friends of mine, who were the drivers of their criminal acts. The mothers in Shakespeare are almost never positive, whereas the daughters and lovers are: they're capable of sacrificing themselves for love. Sometimes, it's for the love of an indecisive prince who has fallen prey to his nightmares, who wavers about in desperation: to command or not to command, to repent or not to repent, to fight or not to fight...never to decide. In the Quartieri, Hamlet is afraid of everybody.

We're the kings of contraband, and they call us bosses, Mafiosi, Camorristi, but they could just as well call us Macbeth, Hamlet, Antonio. Shakespeare had seen this stuff over and over again. This is why he can help a criminal open his eyes. He opened my eyes to the only options I've ever had: run for my life, take the oath and join their ranks, or turn and face them head-on. In other words, you can run away from it all, you can go over to the enemy's side, or you can attack. I never went over to the enemy's side and perhaps this is the only reason I got through it all alive.

That and because theatre has taught me to understand and to forgive.

It's at this point that sleep comes.

In the end it turns out that I'm not the one who has to give Carminati the group's reply: before he and his sidekicks reappear in the kitchen during food delivery time, a European conference on prisons, held at Rebibbia itself, gives us the chance to meet up in the same room as delegations from all the other sections of the prison. And what do you know, in the front line at the conference is our very own 'political' prisoner, the guy who's studied. Cosimo takes the initiative and walks up to him.

'You got something to say to me?' he asks. I'm watching them from a short distance, but I can hear what they're saying and I'm ready to intervene if need be. They stare at each other like cowboys preparing for a duel.

'Didn't your mates pass on what I said?' Carminati replies.

'Don't send me any more messages.' Cosimo doesn't beat around the bush. 'We don't want anything to do with people like you.'

Carminati squares his shoulders and opens his mouth to reply, but Cosimo freezes him on the spot: 'We know all about what you lot are doing in here,' he adds. 'We don't like you as a man, and we don't like your politics. You need to leave us alone otherwise we will come down and split your head open.'

Carminati looks around him and his eyes meet mine. I can read a question on his face: How much do these guys know? And he's well aware that we have the warden's trust.

We already know what's going to come out in the news-papers in just a few weeks' time: that he and his gang have transformed section G8 of the prison into an oasis of freedom and illegality: drugs, parties, mobile phones, corruption…But in maximum security, where we are, it's all school, theatre and gardening. We're even set up for university study now—guys can get a degree in here. We run a call centre: we administer all the fines that are given in Rome, and we also look after the Telecom Italia information line: when people phone up, we're the ones telling them where to find a pharmacy that's open, or the nearest bar. The man giving out that information is doing it from inside a prison. That's the way forward. Not carrying on your own business interests and your own wars in prison, but taking justice and forgiveness to the outside. No Macbeth, with all his ambition, will be our leader; no Richard III, with all his bitterness. Like Richard, Carminati has decided 'to prove a villain, and hate the idle pleasures of these days'. But for us, those pleasures are what will save us.

'What are you looking at?' Carminati growls at me. 'Are you the one coming to split my head open?'

At this point the old Sasà would reply: 'I don't have to wait. I'll split your head open right now, just to confirm that there's nothing inside it.' And the old Sasà would be more than ready to move from words to actions. But that would mean starting a war.

I don't move a muscle, and I hold my rage at bay. I call to my aid, to lend me some words, a man whose greatness many do not understand.

'Had you rather Caesar were living, and die all slaves, than that Caesar were dead, to live all freemen?' I ask, stepping away from the wall and straightening up. 'As Caesar loved me, I weep for him; as he was fortunate, I rejoice at it; as he was valiant, I honour him: but, as he was ambitious, I slew him.'

According to Dante, Brutus was a murderer, a traitor. According to Shakespeare, he was a brave man who did what had to be done. I'm with Shakespeare. If I can avoid it, I will, but like Brutus, I will do what has to be done.

I look around, hoping the message has got through: to Carminati, to his men, to everyone else. If someone threatens our project, we'll defend ourselves.

'Who is here so vile that will not love his country? If any, speak, for him have I offended,' I add, casting my eyes around the room. After a moment of silence, one of the prisoners starts to clap. And then another, and another. Soon the applause is thunderous. It's a vote of confidence in us. The people have declared victory, and have done so in the name of theatre.

I smile, even at Carminati, who's looking at me in astonishment. He knows he has lost, and I know that he won't be making any more advances towards us.

I give my audience a slight nod as the applause dies down.

This is without doubt the best way I've ever found to prevent a war from starting.

11

You're wrong, dear Samuel. There's nothing funny about unhappiness.

I put the book down, annoyed. Today is one of those days when I disagree with Beckett. He was recommended to me by Bennett, who is a huge fan. I didn't like *Waiting for Godot*, but he persuaded me to try again with *Endgame*.

'Beckett is a genius,' he told me. 'He's not easy at first, but once you understand him, he'll open up your mind.'

'Beckett doesn't open up a thing,' I replied. 'Beckett's doing a life sentence.'

I'm even more convinced of this now I'm reading *Endgame*. Beckett's locked up in his cell—which contains another cell, and another one again, like a set of Chinese boxes—telling the same story over and over because it's the only one he's got. He repeats something to you until you understand that that's the way it is, and it couldn't be any other way, and then he turns it all around so that in reality it can't be that way, and yet it is. He's like someone who's banging himself back and forth from one wall of his cell to the other, endlessly. Some days it hurts physically to read him.

And yet I read and re-read him because he's also doing me good: he's showing me the absurdity of life and the traps of my mind. He's making me see how stupid I've been. His writing contains my past self, and reading it is like locking yourself in a dark room to reflect.

Except that I've been in a dark room for a pretty long time now—isn't it about time I came out? I pick up my copy of *The Tempest*, almost with relief. If Beckett is the black box that helps you understand why the plane crashed, Shakespeare's the one who shows you the plane as it's falling and explains to you, as though in a dream, that you have the capacity to change direction. If Beckett closes a door behind me so that I can reflect, Shakespeare shows me a thousand doors, explains which one I came through and must never open again, and then gives me the chance to choose between the others.

Freedom. It's a word that continues to hurt. The doors will never open for me.

I close the book, feeling uneasy. Luckily, it's time to head down—today I'm on the team in the kitchen again, checking that the meat's the right colour. But I'm nervous and distracted. I barely even say hello to Gaetano as I pass him. He's offended, and I feel guilty: *Manners, Sasà. It's hardly Gaetano's fault you've had an argument with Beckett.* Downstairs I come upon another of the regular prisoners, a face I've seen before. I offer him my hand, determined to snap myself out of this dark mood and be polite.

But when he takes my hand he grips it and doesn't let go. He continues holding it so tight that he's trembling. What's happening to him? I take a better look at him.

He's one of those lot: in here for sex crimes. I've always nodded hello to him, because he would look at me insistently and I don't want any trouble, but I'd never have dreamed of shaking the hand of someone like that. I really am distracted today. I wrench my hand from his.

'What's up with you?' I ask.

'Nothing. I'm just happy that you shook my hand,' he replies, with tears in his eyes.

'I shake everybody's hand,' I say abruptly. I'm trying to play down the significance of the gesture, but at the same time I feel a little ashamed. Could my handshake make such a difference to another human being's life? I'd never even realised. When all's said and done, we're in the same boat: he's an inmate like me.

'You've never shaken my hand,' he says.

I'm about to ask why that should matter but I keep quiet.

Clearly it matters a lot. This man noticed—since when? Weeks ago? Months?—that I come down, greet each person with a handshake, but just nod and say hi to him.

I look at him a bit more closely: his face is half hardened, half humble.

'Caliban,' I say, without even thinking.

The prison rapist is Caliban. (Caliban, in fact, tried to rape Miranda.) The man I'm talking to is a prisoner on the second floor who we usually don't even want to look at, who we call the worst names day after day and threaten to kill.

He's Caliban.

And yet we're no better than him. Sure, men like him committed disgusting crimes, but who do we think we are, the good guys? Hardly. From the depths to which we've sunk, who are we to judge what is the more disgusting crime?

Ariel doesn't reject Caliban. He finds a way to live with him. And Prospero isn't ruthless towards Caliban, but keeps a watchful eye on him and tries to rehabilitate him, to civilise him. I can keep away from certain people, but I can't treat them ruthlessly.

We'll never be good people until we stop judging others. Caliban is our touchstone: if our reactions towards him are balanced, it means that the process is bearing fruit. This character—though I never liked him—is indispensable: he is someone to measure ourselves against; he shows us what we're becoming.

I've got to explain this to the guys as soon as I can. I'll tell them at rehearsal. In the meantime, I give the rapist a slap on the back.

'Come on, let's go check this meat.'

He follows me meekly, reconciled with the world. I know that from this point on I can never take that handshake away from him. And nor would I want to.

'Ma'am, just follow my reasoning on this for a moment.' I'm standing before the section head again—by now she must be cursing the day they brought me into this place (not as much as I am, though).

'What is it this time, Striano?' she asks, glancing anxiously at the huge books I've placed on her table. They're all damaged, like books that have been leafed through a lot, eaten and drunk and cursed and lived with. They're the first books I picked up in all my life, and even now, distracted though I am by all the others, I've never stopped reading these ones.

'I'm here to tell you why you have to put me in with the regulars,' I reply, thumping the cover of the Penal Code.

Since arriving in Italy I've tried a number of times to cut down my sentence. In my opinion—but also, I discovered, according to the law—different crimes are paid for individually, not bundled into the one sentence. But in my case they took four convictions and put them on one account, one single sentence, with a total of fourteen years. Easy, isn't it?

Easy, my arse. In Italy there are a number of different imprisonment regimes. They can't just stick you in under one regime, whichever one suits them, and then throw away the key. Five of the years I was sentenced to were for regular crimes, so why should I serve time for those ones in maximum security? With regular crimes, you have the right to request privileges, like rewards for good behaviour and even early release, but you can't do that with more serious crimes: Camorristi don't get any of those privileges. One article that I found was cited in my conviction, Article 4b, prohibits granting such privileges to certain prisoners, those found to be a 'social menace'. To work out that I was socially menacing I had to change codes, because this is not in the Penal Code but in the Penitentiary Regulations. I read there that to be able to drop 4b, to get it removed from your conviction, I'd have to collaborate with justice.

'Ma'am, why have I still got 4b?' I'd asked her in one of our previous meetings.

'Because you haven't collaborated,' she replied, as though it was obvious.

'How can you say I'm not collaborating?'

'Striano, don't play dumb. How have you been collaborating with justice?'

'What, so doing theatre, working, studying, that's not collaborating?' On this occasion I got heated talking to her. 'Do you remember who I used to be? What I used to do? Have you read my file thoroughly?'

'Striano, it doesn't work that way,' she sighed. 'Collaborating means naming your accomplices.'

'But they're all in jail—they're in more trouble than I am...'

'You still have to name names.'

I thought about it briefly, and decided not to do it. I was no longer capable of something like that—I'm not sure I ever had been. Besides, I want to do my prison time differently. I don't want to become an informer, especially on top of all the other trouble I've already been in. So that day I withdrew quietly and continued studying and filing petitions. Eventually the Court of Naples declared I was right, determining that I've served my sentence for the crime of association, and now only the regular crimes remain. The court cut down my sentence and reclassified the crime I was still inside for.

So here I stand before the section head. I take a deep breath and launch into my closing argument like I'm some hotshot lawyer.

'Ma'am, I've served my time for criminal association: three years. I've also served my time for Article 7, extortion: four years. That makes seven. I've got another seven years left, but if we consider sentence reductions, that comes down to four years.' I've studied so much and filed so many petitions that I've actually been able to get my sentence reduced from fourteen years and eight months to eleven years and ten months. 'So, can I now serve the remaining four years in with the regulars?' I ask in conclusion.

The section where regular prisoners are held is the antechamber to freedom. You get released from there, not here—nobody's ever been released directly from maximum security. I look at her thinking, like Ariel, *I want my freedom.*

Haven't I done enough for you? Theatre, gardening, study…I've done everything possible and more—I've done the unimaginable. Give me my freedom.

'Striano, you can't go in with the regulars.' This is a stab to the guts. Prison is a place where eight words are enough to shatter your every hope. 'Your interpretation of the code is wrong,' the section head adds, allowing no right of appeal. 'You're a high-security inmate; even if you went in with the regulars you'd be going as a member of a criminal gang, a Camorrista.'

'I'm sorry, but are you making up an internal law?' I ask. 'Because this isn't written in any of these books.' I thump the cover again, as though the words inside, however cold and complicated they are, might give me comfort.

'Striano,' she says sharply. 'Do this: file your petition directly to the warden. Don't file it to me, because I won't accept it.'

Her tone is harsh as she dismisses me. It's as though the issue is not sufficiently important to deserve any more of her time. But do you have any idea, ma'am, how many goddamn hours I've spent sweating over those codes? Do you know how much hope I've invested in this meeting, how many sleepless hours? Don't you know that *I'm right?*

I stand up.

'Don't worry, I won't file the petition again,' I say, as brusque and cold as her. 'Not to you, not to the warden. No inconvenience, no communication. I'll stay shut up in my cell, I won't talk to anybody anymore. No more work, no more study, no more theatre. I'll stay there until the four years have passed and you turn the key and let me out.'

She looks at me speechless. Then she smiles and shakes her head. And she says something she really shouldn't say: 'Come on, Striano, I know you're a good actor, but don't put on a show for me now.'

'Don't worry,' I reply through clenched teeth. How dare she treat me so unjustly and then laugh at me? 'No more shows.'

Maybe she realises she's overdone it, because the next day Gaetano comes to get me.

'Sasà, the section head wants to see you.'

I don't even look up from my book.

'Sasà, are you deaf? Put your book down for a minute, the section head wants to see you!'

This guy doesn't get it unless you write it on the wall for him in big letters. I look up and our eyes meet, but I don't move. I put my finger to my closed lips, to show him I won't say a single word. Then I continue reading. Silence strike.

I can sense him hesitating, but he doesn't argue—he knows me too well. I hear his footsteps fading into the distance. I continue staring at the page, unable to decipher a thing—it is Beckett, after all—as the rage and frustration building up become too much for me. Do they think they can pacify me? Do they think they can bend me to their will? All I ask for is justice. I demand it.

Only half an hour goes by and I hear footsteps approaching. Has he come back to get me? Whatever, I'm not moving.

'Striano.'

I jump. It's the section head. She's never come to the cells before—a woman in the corridors?

'So what do we have to do, Striano?' she persists.

I look at her without replying, like I did with Gaetano.

'Striano! I'm talking to you! I'll file a disciplinary report against you!' She raises the tone of her voice. This must be quite the performance for those in the neighbouring cells.

'Don't talk to me. I don't want to lose my manners,' I finally say, since she won't stop yelling. Then I plunge back into silence and turn my back.

After a moment I hear her leave.

I know why they don't want to put me in with the regulars. It's got nothing to do with codes, or with the interpretation of the law. It's not because of what I did, but because of what I'm doing in here. The guards are sneaking in to watch me rehearse and giving me reviews when they see me in the corridors—they say I'm a real talent. The inmates come to me to ask what activities they should get involved in, so they can get something noted down in their file about their progress towards rehabilitation. Each inmate needs to work on this file because, if he's diligent, after seven or eight years he'll be able to apply for some privileges, a bit more light in his cell, three days at home, five days, a breath of fresh air. This whole file business is really important...

'Have you done nothing these past seven years?' they can ask, if it turns out you haven't participated, haven't signed up for activities. And I feel like saying to them in reply, 'So what if that's the case? Isn't nothing enough for you? For a guy who's caused only trouble all his life to have got through seven years doing nothing—that's a thing in itself.'

In any case, I haven't done nothing. In fact, I've done a hell of a lot. Too much. And now they won't let me leave.

He's too useful a servant, Ariel, on an island hosting untrustworthy types. This lot have become fond of me because I know how to act, I'm good at washing floors, I'm good at reading… but I'm no longer interested. I need to get out of this place. And the only way to do it is to move in with the regulars.

I spend four days in complete silence, shut up in my cell, while outside the floors gather dirt because I'm no longer washing them, and the inmates' wives wait in vain for their love letters, and the theatre company waits in vain for me. At the end of the fourth day Gaetano arrives.

'Sasà, the section head said to take you down to where the regulars are.'

He doesn't seem happy, and I'm pleased that he's sorry I'm leaving, but apart from that, all I feel is a deep sense of justice. Not victory, because this wasn't a war, but justice, because I asked for and was granted my rights, like any citizen of this country, of this world. Not an outcast, a citizen.

When I come back to rehearsal there's only one day to go until my transfer to the other section. Cavalli's hair is standing on end.

'What have you done? Are you going to tell me what the hell got into you? Did you really ask for a transfer?'

There's a mumbling among the others too, a mix of

amazement, envy and dismay.

'I'd been requesting it for months,' I say, without apology. 'And they've finally granted it.'

'But Sasà, surely you know that you can't come in here from the regular section to do theatre?' Cavalli is almost shouting.

'I'll apply for access to maximum security in order to participate in theatre,' I shrug, pretending to be sure of myself.

'You know perfectly well they're not going to allow that!'

Actually, I do. Or at least I suspect it. The different sections are completely sealed off from each other—what kind of maximum security would it be, otherwise? It's not like inmates can visit each other like little old ladies at teatime, or go back and forth for stage rehearsal.

'Sasà, it's six days to the performance!' Cavalli starts back up again. He almost has tears in his eyes. 'Withdraw your application. Ask them to keep you here!'

I look at him, and then at all the others, one by one. I'm sorry, I really am. But if I back down now they'll never transfer me, I'm sure of it. This is my chance to make that essential step towards reaching the end of my jail term.

'You see, Fabio,' I say, 'I'm Ariel.'

'Huh?' he looks at me confused.

'I'm Ariel,' I repeat. 'I must have my freedom.'

I know the others understand. If they were in my position they'd choose to go down the same road. But that doesn't make it any easier to do what I have to do: turn my back on everyone and leave.

12

'If I have too austerely punished you,
Your compensation makes amends, for I
Have given you here a third of mine own life,
Or that for which I live.'

Prospero in *The Tempest*
Act IV, Scene I

The atmosphere is electric behind the curtain, which remains closed.

I did it. Or perhaps Cavalli did it, I don't know. Finding another Ariel in five days—and I reckon even if they'd had more time—was impossible, so the warden gave permission for me to go back into the maximum-security section, just for rehearsals and the performance.

'Provided you're always escorted by the guards,' he insisted, trying to look stern.

I looked from him to the guard.

'Sir, it doesn't cost me anything to be escorted,' I said. 'But I spent years up there. I know everybody. What do you think I'm likely to get up to? What's changed? It's not like you gave me superpowers by putting me in with the regulars. You just guaranteed me some rights, some privileges: it's a little step forward, and it's one that I earned.'

The passion in my voice surprised him, but in that moment I was Ariel. Ariel who had nothing against an escort, but who was tired of being in chains.

'What has changed, really?' the guard said, cautiously backing me up.

'What's changed is that we're creating a precedent, putting a regular inmate in with those in maximum security,' the warden replied, as severe as Prospero.

But because he's also as generous and just as Prospero, here I am now, checking over the set—bunk beds and twisted sheets rigged up all over the place—pacing nervously back and forth in the wings.

'All good?' Fabione asks, seeing that I look worried. He's holding his bucket—a giant metal thing that looks no bigger than a coffee cup in his hands.

Fabione is a colossus, a wardrobe of a man with shoulders as wide as a major highway, who—no kidding—has to go through the doors of the prison sideways. That's why when his mother died and his morale was very low, everyone was worried he'd cause havoc. So they called me at once, and I dragged him into the theatre group. He can't act to save himself, but I gave him a bucket and I said, 'Fabione, you'll play...the tempest.'

And our *Tempest* begins, in fact, with him beating on his bucket like there's no tomorrow. There are several drummers in the show, making an unimaginable racket, but Fabione is the most vigorous of them all. Shakespeare therapy worked on him, too, and he's as grateful to me as if I'd saved his life. I give him a thumbs up. I know it's important to him. This is the crazy thing about theatre, it brings you closer to other people, it makes you more human. Because without others, and without the company, you can't do a thing on stage. Sure, you can do a monologue, but it's not the same thing. At the end, the audience leaves, but the company sticks with you after the show.

That's why I've put a lot of work into finding more members for the theatre group, to get them out of their cells. I tell them that even in here you can find a life, a direction, a new way of thinking. Spending time outside of their cells is a way of getting out of their heads, and away from that lovesickness, which is really nostalgia, for a world that seems lost. See, prison is also a state of mind, something inside your head, so that's the first place you need to drive it out of.

'What foul play had we that we came from thence? Or blessed wast we did?' says the sweet voice of Miranda, now on stage.

Huh, I think, looking around me at each of these men as they pace nervously, mumbling their lines. Was it a tragedy, ending up in here, or a blessing in disguise? Would we have

180

found ourselves if we hadn't first found the island that is prison, and on it this other island that is the theatre?

'I can't remember a thing,' says Lello, grabbing me by the arm. 'Nothing. Not a single line.'

'Neither can I,' I reply, and it's true. I can't reassure him. Instead he's just aggravating my own anxiety. He knows perfectly well, as do I, that the problem is just those ten minutes before you go on stage, and that once you're in front of the audience the lines will come naturally, as though we'd invented them that very moment. We've been working towards this for months.

But dammit, it's a full house out there. Five hundred seats filled with people from the outside, not only our own families, but also newspapers and television reporters. It's crammed full of VIPs. I'm nervous. My mental blank is worse than usual, and I'm trying to think about my lines but not one of them is coming to me. Help. This time I really can't remember. It's all gone. I know that looking at the script is not the solution. In fact it would only make me panic more, because suddenly the words would look strange, unfamiliar. I can only detach myself from the others, step inside myself and find silence, order. Find a space for Ariel.

Then it is time to go on stage and I'm a whirlwind.

The applause that breaks out reaches the heavens. It thrills me and it gives me strength. I dance, I leap, I climb up on to the bunk beds, I clutch on to the sheets, leaning out perilously.

o

The words flow through my mind and my lips like music:

All hail, great master; grave sir, hail! I come
To answer thy best pleasure be't to fly,
To swim, to dive into the fire, to ride
On the curled clouds.

And I leap in front of Cosimo and glance furtively at him with Ariel's mix of impudence and hope, as he sternly gives his orders. But it's still Cosimo glaring at me, not Prospero. The others told me he celebrated when I left to move in with the regulars. I hadn't realised he had such an issue with me, that he was so annoyed by everybody's affection towards me, and especially their habit of coming to me for advice. But deep down I shouldn't be surprised: for Cosimo, theatre's only about the spectacle: a handful of Camorristi trained like monkeys. For me, for the rest of us…it has become our lives.

'Thou did promise to bate me a full year,' I remind him. The words almost stick in my throat, as they always do.

'Dost thou forget from what a torment I did free thee?' Cosimo roars, more forceful than is necessary. But that's the only way he knows how to play Cosimo: inflexible and angry. He's the same with Caliban, who is the next one to fall victim to his rage, shortly afterwards, as I watch from the wings.

'Thou most lying slave, whom stripes may move, not kindness! I have used thee, filth as thou art, with human care, and lodged thee in mine own cell, till thou didst seek to violate the honour of my child.'

I wonder if the audience is aware that we're talking about ourselves here, that nothing is more real than the human dynamics this play depicts. From Naples down, Shakespeare's on home territory. In the north of Italy, maybe things are different. Maybe families and social networks there don't get as caught up in crime. Sure, in the north there are intrigues among the powerful, but it's permissible not to greet your neighbour. You don't even have to know your neighbour. But in Naples, you must know your neighbour, be it as friend or enemy, and you must find a way to enter that person's life and keep them under control. Surveillance and punishment, like Prospero with Caliban. One or the other, or both at once. In Calabria, there are still shops where, if a policeman comes in, they'll spit on the ground and snarl, 'You're not welcome in here.' What is that if not Shakespearean theatre in its purest form? What sort of a tragedy is it, where a uniformed officer, a man who serves the state, can't come in and buy a bottle of water or ask the owner if everything's all right? Is it life, or theatre?

It's both. And we inmates are like Caliban: deformed, violent, capable only of dark, twisted thoughts. But we can't be kept here, on this island, just to serve our sentence. We're here to learn the power of language, and to learn forgiveness.

'Do so, and after two days I will discharge thee.' The first time Prospero promises me freedom is always the most painful, because I know all too well that almost the entire play has to run before he actually comes good on his word. It's the only moment when I wish it would all be over. I focus on my first task as Ariel: I must save the lives of Alonso and Gonzalo when Sebastian and Antonio plot to kill them.

'Draw together, and when I rear my hand, do you the like to fall it on Gonzalo,' says Antonio maliciously. These guys are proud to be playing the nastiest characters in the whole play: they're slowly coming to terms with everything they've done in their lives.

For me, they are the two hardest characters to forgive. They're not just wicked, they're also arrogant in their wickedness. I compare them to the politicians I see tearing each other to bits on television. I'd like to ask those politicians: aren't you ashamed of yourselves? Where do you get all this brazenness? For you, words have no value, and that means you have no real power. You'll only stay on your throne as long as the people are listening to you. And if tomorrow we're not, we can get rid of you in two minutes flat. All it takes is a little revolution, an uprising. It's the citizens who make a country great, if they observe the laws and value the land. But if you lot think you can change things on your own, if you think that you alone with your words can summon up a tempest, then you're nuts.

'You fools! I and my fellows are ministers of fate.' I'm more solemn than usual when I begin my speech to the dumbfounded bad guys, the 'men of sin' of the play; I'm telling them that their swords can do nothing to us, because we're spirits of the air, protected by Prospero who, unlike them, has true power: the power to forgive.

The play is coming to an end and it's as though my mind

has split in half. I'm entirely Ariel in one part, but when Ariel's not on stage I'm Sasà, following breathlessly, worrying when someone's on the verge of forgetting a line, prompting him under my breath, giving congratulatory slaps on the back. We haven't forgotten that we're prisoners on a journey, not real actors who've been through drama school. Our faces can't help but flush with colour, and our eyes can't help but well up with tears, when we relate so closely to the lines we're saying. Perhaps this is why, when I asked Prospero for my freedom in Act One, and I paused, the audience applauded. They're on my side.

This guy wants freedom. He's asking you for it with all his heart. Give it to him, they're thinking. They're on my team. From the depths of prison I invoke freedom, and there's not a single person in the room who doesn't know how cruel that is; how necessary.

Soon they're applauding every time I come on stage and at the end of each of my lines, meaning I have to keep pausing until they fall quiet again. A connection has formed between the audience and me. I can feel them. I'm gazing beyond them, at the tempest, at the island and all its perils, but I can feel their eyes on me, their breath, their positive energy bouncing off mine and pushing me onwards.

They know me and appreciate me in a way I've never experienced before. Back when I was on the outside, people would recognise that I had certain qualities. But I didn't like those people. I didn't even like winning a turf war—it was just a victory that brought with it more trouble. *Don't dress me up in this poison, this bitterness*—I used to think when people would greet me in the Quartieri—because I did what I did to stop the war, not gain glory from it. And don't think I did it because I'm the good guy, the handsome, honourable one, the Robin Hood of the back alleys as my mother would have it, the man who can't stand by and tolerate injustice, the abuse of power, bullying—that's not who I am. I'm a criminal.

But even I can be forgiven.

'For you, most wicked sir, whom to call brother would even infect my mouth, I do forgive thy rankest fault—all of them.' The forgiveness Prospero grants his brother is like a slap in the face, because the greatest revenge is forgiveness. This kind of forgiveness can offend. Prospero doesn't tell him he forgives him, that everything's fine and all has been forgotten, because that would be hypocrisy at its purest. But presenting him with the bill, and then treating him with indifference, is how to make an enemy pay the highest price. You rob him of the honour of a knifing, the satisfaction of a duel. You render him insignificant and you exclude him from your life.

That line always sends shivers down my spine, because it's the high point of Prospero's greatness. But more than that, because I know what comes next.

'Come hither, spirit. Set Caliban and his companions free; untie the spell,' the sorcerer commands me. He generously bestows freedom on all his island's reluctant guests.

My heart is thumping. I'm obsessed with this moment that comes at the end of the play. I know it's not healthy, but I can't help myself. When do I get my freedom? In every rehearsal, for months, I've been asking that of Prospero the way I'd ask a judge, a prison official, a guard. When you are in prison, that word is so cruel. You can't ask a prisoner to keep saying it again, and again, and again. It's not only me who feels this— when I used to practise my lines in the common areas, the sound of those two syllables used to irritate others, too. I remember once a Neapolitan guy asking me to shut up, his eyes full of pain, saying, 'Mate, I've got twenty years. Can you give it a rest?'

'Yeah, yeah, sorry.' How could I explain to him that freedom is not on the outside, freedom is right in here, if you have it inside of you. How could I explain that in treading these boards I am already free, and yet, it is now even more painful to not be entirely free.

For weeks now they've been talking about a pardon. We watch the 6 p.m. news and follow the progress of the law through parliament. Radio Radicale has never been so popular inside Rebibbia Prison. We see the pardon approaching, but we don't know if it's a mirage. And I'm afraid even to hope. I can't take it anymore. I've had enough of acknowledging what I did wrong, of rehabilitation—I want out.

When Prospero speaks, my heart quivers.

'My Ariel, chick, that is thy charge. Then to the elements be free, and fare thou well!'

Tears well up in my eyes, more unstoppable than during any rehearsal. It's the magic of the stage: all those held breaths, all those eyes fixed upon me. *You're all witnesses*, I think. *He's given me back my freedom.*

When Prospero takes two steps forward to do the final monologue, I discreetly dry my eyes, but it's pointless. When the lights come up and we move downstage, the tears start to flow, one at a time at first, and then all together, faster than ever. I can see, sitting in the front row, and also crying without restraint, don Pasquale. He is clapping hard enough to flay his own hands. This man who I don't think has ever shouted in his life is smiling widely and shouting 'Bravo!'.

As I bow to the audience, the applause drowning me is louder than it is for anyone else, and I briefly imagine the whole theatre will fall down, and the prison will collapse with it and we'll find ourselves standing among the rubble under the open sky, free.

To the elements be free.

Except the only place I'm going is back to my cell.

It's over all too soon—the applause, the handshakes from so many, including the warden's wife, who comes to the edge of the stage with her daughter to congratulate me. 'My husband has spoken so much about you, but I didn't expect you to be that good. Congratulations!'

I'm moved by her praise, but a second later I can no longer see or hear her. Behind her I've spotted Monica, a little off to the side, almost holding back, as though she can't believe her eyes and is struggling to recognise her Sasà under the bright lights. I move into a quieter corner of the stage and gesture to her to come over. I bend down towards her. She still has tears running down her face. I dry one with my finger.

'How is it possible that I always manage to make you cry, even when I'm being good?' I'm trying to make a joke but my voice is trembling.

'Sasà, you were fantastic…It didn't seem like you.' She, too, forces a smile.

My finger on her cheek becomes a caress.

'Oh, so when I'm fantastic you don't recognise me? Thanks a lot!'

She laughs, a little reassured by my usual lighthearted manner. But as I touch her, it's as though beneath my fingers I can sense the signs of my absence. That 'it didn't seem like you' has pierced me like a poison arrow. Am I still me? Is she still Monica? Our love, in the midst of all the violence, all the fear, all the mistakes, has always stayed pure, I'm convinced of that. Now, in the magic light of the theatre, which reveals things as they really are, the sentiment we share seems to me to be wounded, laboured. Will it survive separation?

'Sasà!'

'Don Pasquale!' My cell neighbour has appeared alongside my wife, saving me from the intensity of a question I don't wish to ask myself right now. 'Did you like me in the show? I hope I did you the honour of living up to what you taught me.'

My tone is still playful. Maybe it's just a way of putting up a wall to defend myself. But don Pasquale doesn't want walls, and he doesn't laugh.

'I've missed you since you left for the regulars,' he says.

'I miss you, too, don Pasquale,' I reply, no longer trying to joke around. 'I have no one to talk poetry with down there.'

'Soon you'll have as many as you want,' he replies.

'Why? Do you know of a gang of criminal poets that's about to be sent down?'

'You'll be the one getting out. You'll be out soon.' His dark eyes are fixed on me, as though he can see deep inside me, or perhaps something even well beyond me. 'We won't meet again. I'll miss you.'

'That's not funny, don Pasquale,' I exclaim, almost frightened. 'It'll be another four years before I'm free…'

'Sasà, you've already gained your freedom. You're free.' As he speaks these words, his voice is that of Prospero, I'm sure of it. And the hand clasping mine is the hand of the sorcerer, bidding farewell to his Ariel.

I can't stop myself. I burst into tears, jump down off the stage and hug him tightly. Gaetano, alarmed, rushes up to separate us.

'Sasà, what are you doing? You're not allowed down among the audience, you know that!'

'Goodbye, don Pasquale,' is all I can say before I have to get back up onto the stage, choking back the tears. The guards are already moving us, gently but firmly, back into the wings. We have to go back to our cells. Our little meet-and-greet only lasted a few minutes, and we're granted no time to celebrate among ourselves. The guards lock us back up again, the rest of the cast in maximum security and me with the regulars.

I look down at the ground as I walk and after the torrent of emotions that suddenly rushes through me, my heart turns to mush and I can't even feel it beating. After the fear, the excitement, the emotion, I'm filled with a disappointed rancour. One more we've let them abort our emotions. Why didn't they let us stay? Why didn't they let us down among the audience?

The praise from everyone is like medicine to me. At the end of the performance it wasn't solidarity I saw on their faces, but admiration. And whereas solidarity can take the form of toxic reverence from false friends like I had in the Quartieri, admiration is something that fills a human being with positive energy. Solidarity is fine at a local level, but in here we need to be shaken up. Something needs to explode within us, killing the black wolf and allowing the white wolf to win, because otherwise we'll never get out.

My cell is as silent as the grave.

I fling my script into the corner, enraged. The tiny window offers a square of sky that is too dark and too small. If I squint, I think I can see just one single star in that infinite depth. If I was lucky, it would be my star.

I stare at that light as though it might hypnotise me and take my mind out of here.

'Shakespeare,' I murmur. I feel as though only he, maybe, is listening to me tonight. 'Shakespeare, I recited your words. I did honour to your genius. But this performance hurts too much— talking about freedom every day is a kind of torture.' I take a deep breath and summon up my voice, like I do on stage. If they hear me in the neighbouring cells, who cares, I've talked with my mother, with Dante, with Macbeth, with Beckett, so now I'm going to talk to Shakespeare—I reckon that's the least of it.

'Shakespeare, give me my freedom. Give it to me now. If you truly give it back to me, I promise to give you ten years of my life. Ten years in which I'll take your philosophy—of giving, doing, loving—out into the world. Ten years during which I'll take the truest emotions of mankind and put them on stage, and in your words. Because what we need today is someone who can help people interpret the world, and artists need to go out among the people and teach life.'

I clench my fists, concentrating on the winking of that minuscule star, bright and indomitable, like my hope.

'I promise to be there, Shakespeare. I'll be wherever I can be of service—in prisons, in schools. In the streets and right in the midst of the evils of the earth and I'll be afraid of nothing, ashamed of nothing, and there will be words for all, and forgiveness for all. But give me my freedom. Give me my freedom.'

INTERMEZZO

Nobody is nothing. Nothing doesn't exist. If you're alive, even if you're in prison, it's because you're something. And you have to know who you are. You have to know what you've done. You have to know there's a price to pay for evil; you certainly can't expect applause. But you also have to know that things could have gone, and could still go, differently.

We're the school bullies, the ones who skipped school and then stopped going altogether. We're the leaders of unjust causes. Each of us carries his story inside him, and the hope of changing it, if not for the past at least for the future. But we need love, justice and a project.

You say the prisons are overcrowded and I reply: they're crowded with criminals, sure, but emotionally they're deserted. There's no support. We need those elves and spirits that Prospero calls upon: social workers, volunteers, counsellors. That's the kind of magic that works. And books, too. Prospero, who started out as a man of power, became a sorcerer thanks to books, and thanks to the time and freedom he had to study them and make them his own. As a governor, Prospero basically failed. When a man fails he has to leave. He must go on a pilgrimage. You have to step out of your own shoes, give up your role, to be able to understand what's calling you, what's missing. You have to learn that vendetta is pointless, and that going and taking back what's yours is worthless. What's useful is building a new kingdom, here on the island, with new different rules. What's useful is forgiveness.

But forgiveness is not absolution. It's someone showing you the doors and explaining how to open them. That's what love is: the gift of possibility. I needed possibilities. I needed someone who believed in me, someone to bring new materials into the poverty of prison. And that's what the other prisoners need, too, if they are to forge their own destinies. As Shakespeare teaches us, destiny doesn't exist. We are made up of actions and our future is in our hands.

If there's something, some kind of energy, conditioning us, we'll discover it on the other side, when the soul goes to dwell elsewhere. But today we are this: beings capable of looking in the mirror and taking responsibility. If we give ourselves credit when things go well and blame it on destiny when they go badly, then what we are no longer counts. We're just air; there's no substance to our treading the earth. Whereas in reality, the stuff we're made of is actions, reactions, feelings, love, passion and poetry. Peace towards your enemy.

We have to make the effort to forgive, and to be forgiven, not as a favour to ourselves but as a favour to our enemies. Forgiveness belongs to them, not us. Letting yourself be forgiven means allowing someone to regain peace, that peace we took from them. This is Shakespearean forgiveness. This is freedom.

Freedom is a strange word. It can be that script sitting on my bedside table in my cell, which I have to be careful not to spill coffee on, because I'd be damaging my freedom. Freedom is a dangerous thing—it's a stone that can strike and injure. It ought to be respected. Some people have so much of it that they can't even approach you for a hug. Others have so little that just a slap on the back might cause them to swallow it. Everybody finds freedom in something. Some find it in a woman, some in a child; I found it in plays, characters, books. I found it inside a prison. Even while still inside, I was already out. But one Sasà can't move a thing. One of me is not enough. There are so many people we have to help out of prison if we're truly going to change things.

Give freedom to the thousand Ariels locked up in the prisons of the world. Give them the words to ask for it.

PART FIVE

INVENTING THE FUTURE

'We are such stuff
As dreams are made on,
and our little life
Is rounded with a sleep.'

Prospero in *The Tempest*
Act IV, Scene I

13

'Oh happy torment, when my torturer
Doth teach me answers for deliverance!'

Bassanio in *The Merchant of Venice*
Act III, Scene II

The sounds of celebration wake me. In prison, it's similar to the sound of a riot: applause, feet stomping on the ground, pots and pans and other objects banging against the cell bars.

Last night I fell asleep, exhausted, as soon as the adrenaline stopped pounding through my veins, but it was very late and my sleep was more restless than usual.

What time is it? What's happening? I've had just long enough to wonder this when a word reaches my ears; a word that explains everything. It's echoing from mouth to mouth through the corridors: a pardon.

Incredulous, I look towards the cell window. It's the middle of the day. Last night's bright star is no longer visible, but I know it's there. So it was mine, after all.

'Shakespeare has given me grace,' I murmur.

Is it truly possible? Could this be freedom? Four years early?

The tears that had only just dried up start flowing all over again. I can't believe it. I'm afraid even to breathe. What if I'm dreaming? I pinch myself hard to make sure I'm awake and it really hurts.

It's real. They've granted a pardon. By now I know the penal code well enough to know that I'll be among those released early.

Shakespeare has given me freedom and now I owe him ten years of my life. It seems a ludicrously small price to pay.

In the course of a few hours it's confirmed: I'm getting out. It's a matter of a few weeks.

So when the warden suddenly summons me, I'm a bundle of nerves.

Why does he want to see me? This isn't the process. I should be released and that's that. My mind fills with doubts, with bad omens, even. I was once Sasà of the Hotheads. What if they say I'm not getting out after all? What if one of the gang members on the outside became a *pentito* and now there are new accusations against me, a new trial to face, a new sentence?

As I follow the guard along the corridor, all the bad deeds I haven't paid for are running through my head, like the words of a curse. Of course I haven't paid all my debts. Nobody does, at least no habitual criminal. If a guy kills his wife, it's different—he's committed a crime and he pays for it. Not quite the case for someone who, say, gets picked up after his eighth armed robbery and serves a sentence for one, or a drug dealer caught the fourth time round who has nevertheless dealt on three previous occasions. Then again, what if a new witness emerges with evidence of another of his misdeeds, and if he turns up just before a guy's release…Maybe somebody doesn't want me to get out. Maybe they've gathered more evidence against me, to keep me in here. But why? Is it once again because I'm a 'social menace'? Or is because they're wondering if they'll ever find another actor who will bring down the house with his performance?

Shakespeare, you can't have played such a cruel trick on me.

Tell you what. If you have, when I finally do get out I'm going to come looking for you.

'What'd you say?' The guard looks at me in surprise and I realise I said this last bit out loud. He didn't catch the exact words but he picked up on my threatening tone. He looks nervous, suspicious.

That's just what I need, to get myself into more trouble. Calm down, Sasà.

'No, nothing, I was just thinking aloud.' I attempt a reassuring smile, but I'm so anxious, who knows what kind of grimace comes out. 'Do you know why the warden wants to see me?'

'No idea,' he replies, with stony expression. He doesn't know, or more likely doesn't want to tell me. It's bad news for sure.

By the time I enter the warden's office, the desperation has tied me into a knot.

'Sir, has something happened?' I blurt out, without even saying hello, and ignoring his outstretched hand. I'm looking at him the way a man dying of thirst looks at some water just beyond his grasp.

'No, what could've happened?' The astonishment on his face seems genuine, and some of my tension releases. At least enough for me to be able to shake his hand.

'Well, I don't know…' I say weakly.

'Striano, what's the matter? Are you hiding something from me?' he asks, half joking, half suspicious.

'Well, sir, you can imagine…'

I sit down in front of his desk even though he hasn't invited me to, because my legs are about to give way. Maybe everything will actually be all right.

'Striano, I wanted to say goodbye to you the way you deserve, because we've been on an extraordinary journey together,' he says, sitting down and looking at me earnestly. 'And to be quite honest I'm also a little worried, and that's why I wanted to talk to you for a few minutes.'

'Worried about me? Worried about me getting out?'

'Yes, because someone like you…How are you going to manage on the outside?'

'Sir, the question is, how's a man going to manage on the inside, not on the outside,' I reply. I think he's raving. Does he have any idea what I've survived—turf wars in Spain, psychiatric medication in Rebibbia…

'The thing is, in here I felt I could protect you,' he continues. 'The journey we've been on has been a protected one. Sheltered from the world, and all its violence, all its temptations. I'm afraid that once you get out of here you'll go back to your old life. I'm afraid that world will suck you back in. It's not an easy world.'

You're telling me? I think, surprised. At nine years of age a security guard was sticking needles in my hands, at twelve I was stealing watches, at fourteen I was dealing cocaine…

'Sir, are you offering me a job as a guard?' I say, trying to make a joke of it. It's certain that danger awaits me on the outside, but that doesn't strike me as a reason to stay in jail. 'Because, you know, otherwise I'm going to have to leave—the government said so.'

This makes him laugh and he realises he's not making any sense.

'You're right, Striano. What are we talking about? It's normal that you should leave at some point.'

His furrowed brow doesn't relax, though. I can understand him. I'm not just one of his inmates, I'm one of his actors. This place is not just a prison, it's his castle. And from today, the entertainment will be missing from his court.

'Sir, I'm sure of what I need to do,' I try to reassure him. 'But as an honest man, which I consider myself to be, a man of my word, I can assure you of at least one thing. It's true, I'm like an addict who says he'll never use again, only because I didn't like the drugs available in here. It's true that when I go out into the world it's possible I'll find some drug I do like. But I don't think it'll get me into trouble, sir.'

'Drugs won't get you into trouble?' he asks. He doesn't follow.

'No. Because I promise you that theatre is my drug now,' I reply resolutely.

He relaxes, and the lines on his forehead disappear. He stands and offers me his hand again. This time I shake it firmly.

'Striano, I'm sure you'll become a great actor.'

I glance around. My things are all in disarray, scattered around my cell, as though I was heading out to a rehearsal. Instead of...

I snap my toothbrush in half and throw the two pieces on the bed.

This is what you do when you're released—you break your toothbrush so you don't end up back inside. Here's hoping. It can't do any harm.

I put on my backpack, with the few objects I'm taking with me: photos, a folder containing my personal documents, including all of Monica's letters. We'll burn them when I get home: in prison we're all fiercely protective of our women's letters, and some of us are tempted to tear them up to stop a cell-mate reading them, but you don't do it: it's like tearing up love. They're to be burned when you're released, alongside the person who wrote them to you. It symbolises a bad period coming to an end; your words no longer need to be written down, because at last they can be said in person.

I think about the wives of those men I wrote love letters for.

I wonder whether they'll be upset when they learn their husbands are not such poets after all. There's nothing I can do about it. I did what I could to help out.

I say goodbye to the inmates as I walk down the corridor for the last time. I say goodbye to the guards. I'm sorry it's not Gaetano taking me through to the outside, but he works in maximum security...

And here I am back in the reception area.

This is where you enter and where you leave. You go through all the entry procedures in reverse. It's the same as before, but you do it with a smile instead of tears: photographs, fingerprints, signatures on piles of forms. There's one important difference, though: instead of coming in through the dirty side you go out the clean side. There are two different doors, and the exit is as beautiful as the entrance is ugly. When you exit Rebibbia it's like you're stepping out of a *palazzo*. At Poggioreale prison in Naples they go one better—the entrance is underground and the exit is above ground. Can you get any more symbolic than that?

I step outside and find myself in an unremarkable open area in an unremarkable suburb. Even the sky is a uniform, featureless grey.

What was I expecting? Fans and a ticker-tape parade?

You're no Hollywood actor, Sasà, I remind myself. Though I certainly can no longer make my living as a criminal: my face has been in all the papers and on television. If I committed an armed robbery, everyone would be telling the police, 'It was that guy, the actor!' I'm ruined as a dealer, too, but I can live with that. Worst comes to worst I'll be a charming waiter. That's if I can find work, obviously.

I suddenly realise what the warden meant when he said he was worried. I feel lost, like I have no direction. Where do I go now, what do I do? I've got no address, no doors I can knock on. It's not as though anybody gave me instructions for the rest of my life. Not even Shakespeare, not yet anyway.

It dawns on me that on the outside I have nothing, not even theatre. Is this freedom? I'm surrounded by a world that has changed in these last seven years, that's going at a different speed, and I risk getting left behind. I look around to see if something is following me, or someone, perhaps the ghost of one of my old selves.

I have to find a bus to take me to the station, and then a train that will take me to Naples. I haven't told Monica I'm getting out today. I want to give her the most beautiful surprise of her life. But in Naples there are people who want to kill me, who have killed many of my friends.

I set out in the hope of finding a bus stop. Instead I come across a school.

I happen upon it quite suddenly, there are flags out the front and at first I think it's a council building, until I read the sign. It's a senior high school.

Poor things, I think. You're still locked up.

When I think of school I become enraged. I'd like to have a word with a few teachers. I'd like to tell them: I never encountered any good teachers, in all my life. Some of you bring problems from home into the school. And some of you don't understand that one student can have one type of intelligence and another can have a different type, that someone who does badly at maths might be a musical genius and it's your job to move him in that direction. Some of you will dissuade the best leaders in the class from continuing their studies, and in doing so, you'll create criminals. Other teachers will know how to understand them, and might even create the men of tomorrow.

The fact is, we need prisons that are more like schools, and schools that are less like prisons.

But for this to happen, the teachers also need freedom.

Freedom to go into class with a project. Freedom to talk to students, to push them in new directions, to explain the world to them. Freedom to say that there's not one single story, one single study plan, rather that life is study and we each have a story, we just need to understand how to carry it forward, and how to tell it.

In this way, we'll have better future generations that can once more begin to love, share and unite. These days we're all looking for a reason to criticise or accuse. We've lost the capacity to love. We've lost the very meaning of love. We take more pride in looking for the bad in someone than looking for the good, even though everybody makes mistakes, constantly. Even though human beings are designed to make mistakes, and to get up if offered an outstretched hand.

When I realise I've entered the school I'm already halfway up the central staircase. It's strange, like a dream—no students, no teachers, no other staff. Nobody stops me or notices me as I make my way down one of the faded yellow corridors. There's that typical school smell. I stop in front of a door that says 'VA', meaning 'go'. It's actually classroom 5A (it's in Roman numerals), but to me it seems like an omen.

These students will get out in a few months, I think. But they've got to serve their whole sentence, and there's no hope of a pardon.

Who knows if, by the time they leave, anyone will have told them a story, to send them out into the world prepared?

I turn the slightly rusty handle and step through.

Twenty heads turn to look at me. The teacher stares, eyes wide. One of the students is standing out the front, clearly in the middle of being quizzed on something.

I can bestow grace on this poor kid, I think.

'Sit back down,' I say resolutely. 'If you don't mind,' I add in a gentler tone, so as not to seem arrogant. 'And good morning to you all.'

'Who are you? What are you doing here?' asks the young teacher, alarmed, as the boy sits down.

'I'm a man who's come to tell you a story,' and I smile at her, the smile of a true actor.

CPSIA information can be obtained
at www.ICGtesting.com
Printed in the USA
LVHW111025041218
598323LV00004B/2/P